SNOWED IN WITH
THE BILLIONAIRE

SNOWED IN WITH THE BILLIONAIRE

BY
CAROLINE ANDERSON

MILLS & BOON

First published in Great Britain 2013
by Mills & Boon, an imprint of Harlequin (UK) Limited,
Large Print edition 2014
Eton House, 18-24 Paradise Road,
Richmond, Surrey, TW9 1SR

© 2013 Caroline Anderson

ISBN: 978 0 263 24045 0

Harlequin (UK) Limited's policy is to use papers that are natural, renewable and recyclable products and made from wood grown in sustainable forests. The logging and manufacturing processes conform to the legal environmental regulations of the country of origin.

Printed and bound in Great Britain
by CPI Antony Rowe, Chippenham, Wiltshire

For Angela, who gave me insight into the harrowing and difficult issues surrounding adoption, and for all 'the girls' in the Harlequin Romance group for their unstinting help, support, and amazing knowledge. Ladies, you rock!

CHAPTER ONE

'OH, WHAT—?'

All Georgia could see in the atrocious conditions were snaking brake lights, and she feathered the brake pedal, glad she'd left a huge gap between her and the car in front.

It slithered to a halt, and she put on her hazard flashers and pulled up cautiously behind it, trying to see why they'd stopped, but visibility was minimal. Even though it was technically still daylight, she could scarcely see a thing through the driving snow.

And the radio hadn't been any help—plenty of talk about the snow arriving earlier than predicted, but no traffic information about any local holdups. Just Chris Rea, singing cheerfully about driving home for Christmas while the fine, granular snow clogged her wipers and made it next to impossible to see where she was going.

Not that they'd been going anywhere fast. The traffic had been moving slower and slower for the last few minutes because of the appalling visibility, and now it had come to a complete grinding halt. She'd been singing along with all the old classics as the weather worsened, crushing the steadily rising panic and trying to pretend that it was all going to be OK. Obviously her crazy, reckless optimism hard at work as usual. When would she learn?

Then the snow eased fleetingly and she glimpsed the tail lights of umpteen cars stretching away into the distance. Far beyond them, barely discernible in the pale gloom, a faint strobe of blue sliced through the falling snow.

More blue lights came from behind, travelling down the other side of the road and overtaking the queue of traffic, and it dawned on her that nothing had come towards them for some minutes. Her heart sank as the police car went past and the flashing blue lights disappeared, swallowed up by the blizzard.

OK, so something serious had happened, but she couldn't afford to sit here and wait for the emergency services to sort it out with the weather going downhill so quickly. If she wasn't careful she'd end up stranded, and she was *so* nearly home, just five or six miles to go. So near, and yet so far.

The snow swirled around them again, picking up speed, and she bit her lip. There was another route—a narrow lane she knew only too well. A lane that she'd used often as a short cut, but she'd been avoiding it, and not only because of the snow—

'Why we stop, Mummy?'

She glanced in the rear-view mirror and met her son's eyes. 'Somebody's car's broken down,' she said. Or hit another car, but she wasn't going to frighten a two-year-old. She hesitated. She was deeply reluctant to use the lane, but realistically she was all out of options.

Making the only decision she could, she smiled brightly at Josh and crossed her fingers. 'It's OK, we'll go another way. We'll soon be at Grannie and Grandpa's.'

His face fell, tugging her heartstrings. 'G'annie now. I hungry.'

'Yeah, me, too, Josh. We won't be long.'

She turned the car, feeling it slither as she pulled away across the road and headed back the way she'd come. Yikes. The roads were truly lethal and they weren't going to get any better as more people drove on them and compacted the snow.

As she turned onto the little lane, she could feel her heart rate pick up. The snow was swirling wildly around the car, almost blinding her, and even when it eased for a second the verges were almost obliterated.

This wasn't supposed to be happening yet! Not until tonight, after they were safely tucked up with her parents, warm and dry and well-fed. Not out in the wilds of the countryside, on a narrow lane that went from nowhere to nowhere else. If only she'd left earlier…

She checked her mobile phone and groaned. No signal. Fabulous. She'd better not get stuck, then. She put the useless phone away, sucked in a deep breath and kept on driving, inching cautiously along.

Too cautiously. The howling wind was blowing the snow straight off the field to her right and the narrow lane would soon be blocked. If she didn't hurry, she wasn't going to get along here at all, she realised, and she swallowed hard and put her foot down a little. At least in the fresh snow she had a bit more traction, and she wasn't likely to meet someone coming the other way. She only had half a mile at the most to go before she hit the other road. She could do it. She could…

A high brick wall loomed into view on the left, rippling in and out like a ribbon, the snow plastered to it like frosting on a Christmas cake, and she felt a surge of relief.

Almost there now. The ancient crinkle crankle wall ran alongside the lane nearly to the end. It would give her a vague idea of where the road was, if nothing else, and all she had to do was follow it to the bigger, better road which would hopefully be clear.

And halfway along the wall—there it was, looming out of the blizzard, the gateway to a hidden world. The walls curved in on both sides of the imposing entrance, rising up to a pair of massive brick piers topped with stone gryphons, and between them hung the huge, ornate iron gates that didn't shut.

Except that today they were firmly shut.

They'd been painted, too, and they weren't wonky any more, she realised as she slowed to a halt. They'd always hung at a crazy angle, open just enough to squirm through, and that gap had been so enticing to an adventurous young girl out for a bike ride with her equally reckless older brother.

The gryphons guarding the entrance had scared them, mythical beasts with the heads and wings of eagles and the bodies of lions, their talons slashing the air as they reared up, but the gap had lured them in, and inside the wall they'd found a secret adventure playground beyond their wildest imaginings. Acres of garden run wild, with hidden rooms and open spaces, vast spreading trees and a million places to hide.

And in the middle of it all, the jewel in the crown, sat the most beautiful house she'd ever seen. A huge front door with a semi-circular fanlight over it was tucked under a pillared portico that sat exactly in the centre of the house, surrounded perfectly symmetrically by nine slender, elegant sash windows.

Not that you could see all the windows. Half of them were covered in wisteria, cloaking the front and invading the roof, and the scent from the flowers, hanging delicately like bunches of pale lilac grapes against the creamy bricks, had been intoxicating.

It had been empty for years; with their hearts in their mouths, she and Jack had found a way inside through the cellar window and tiptoed round the echoing rooms with their faded grandeur, scaring each other half to death with ghost stories about the people who might have lived and loved and died there, and she'd fallen head over heels in love with it.

And then years later, when her brother had started to hang out with Sebastian, she'd taken him there, too. He'd come over to their house one day to see Jack but he'd been out, so they'd gone out for a bike ride instead. His idea, and she'd jumped at it, and they'd ended up here.

It had been their first 'date', not really a date at all but near enough for her infatuated sixteen-year-old self, and she'd dragged him inside the still-empty house just as she had her brother.

Like her, he'd been fascinated by it. They'd explored every inch of it, tried to imagine what it would have been like to live there in its hey-day. What it would be like to live there now. They'd even fantasised about the furnishings—a dining table so long you could hardly see the person at the other end, a Steinway grand in what had to have been the music room and, in the master bedroom, a huge four-poster bed.

In her own private fantasy, that bed had been big enough for them and all their children to pile into for a cuddle. And there'd be lots of them, the foundation of a whole dynasty. They'd fill the house with children, all of them conceived in that wonderful, welcoming bed with feather pillows and a huge fluffy quilt and zillion-thread-count Egyptian cotton sheets.

And then he'd kissed her.

They'd been playing hide and seek, teasing and flirting and bubbling over with adolescent silliness, and he'd found her in the cupboard in the bedroom and kissed her.

She'd fallen the rest of the way in love with him in that instant, but it had been almost two years before their relationship had moved on and fantasy and reality had begun to merge.

He'd gone away to uni, but they'd seen each other every holiday, spent every waking moment together, and the kisses had become more urgent, more purposeful, and way more grown up.

And then, the weekend after her eighteenth birthday, he'd taken her to the house. He wouldn't tell her why, just that it was a surprise, and then he'd led her up to the master bedroom and opened the door, and she'd been enchanted.

He'd set the scene—flickering candles in the

fireplace, a thick blanket spread out on the moth-eaten carpet and smothered in petals from the wisteria outside the window, the scent filling the room—and he'd fed her a picnic of delicate smoked salmon and caviar sandwiches and strawberries dipped in chocolate, and he'd toasted her in pink champagne in little paper cups with red hearts all over the outside.

And then, slowly and tenderly, giving her time even though it must have killed him, he'd made love to her.

She'd willingly given him her virginity; they'd come close so many times, but he'd always stalled her. Not that day. That day, when he'd finally made love to her, he'd told her he'd love her forever, and she'd believed him because she loved him, too. They'd stay together, get married, have the children they both wanted, grow old together in the heart of their family. It didn't matter where they lived or how rich or poor they were, it was all going to be perfect because they'd have each other.

But two years down the line, driven by ambition and something else she couldn't understand, he'd changed into someone she didn't know and everything had fallen apart. Their dream had turned into a nightmare with the shocking intrusion of a reality she'd hated, and she'd left him, but she'd been devastated.

She hadn't been back here in the last nine years, but just before Josh was born she'd heard on the grapevine that he'd bought it. Bought their house, and was rescuing it from ruin.

She and David had been at a dinner party, and someone from English Heritage was there. 'I gather some rich guy's bought Easton Court, by the way—Sebastian something or other,' he'd said idly.

'Corder?' she'd suggested, her whole body frozen, her mind whirling, and the man had nodded.

'That's the one. Good luck to him. It deserves rescuing, but it's a good job he's got deep pockets.'

The conversation had moved on, ebbing and flowing around her while she'd tried to make sense of Sebastian's acquisition, but David had asked her about him as they were driving home.

'How do you know this Corder guy?'

'He was a friend of my brother's,' she said casually, although she was feeling far from casual. 'His family live in that area.'

It wasn't a lie, but it wasn't the whole truth and she'd felt a little guilty, but she'd been shocked. No, not shocked. Surprised, more than anything. She'd thought he'd walked away from everything connected to that time, as she had, and the fact that he hadn't had puzzled her. Puzzled and fascinated and horrified her, all at once, because of course it was so close to home, so near to her parents.

Too close for comfort.

But a few days later Josh had been born, and then only weeks after that David had died and her whole world had fallen apart and she'd forgotten it. Forgotten everything, really, except holding it all together for Josh.

But every time since then that she'd visited her parents, she'd avoided the lane, just as she had today—until she'd had no choice.

Her heart thudded against her ribs. Was he in there, behind those intimidating and newly renovated gates? Alone? Or sharing their house with someone else, someone who didn't share the dream—

She cut that thought off before she could follow it. It didn't matter. The dream didn't exist any longer, and she'd moved on. She'd had to. She was a mother now, and there was no time for dreaming. She dragged her eyes and her mind away from the imposing gates and the man who might or might not be behind them, flashed her son a smile to remind her of her priorities and made herself drive on.

Except her car had other ideas. It slithered wildly as she tried to pull away, and the snow swirled around them, the wind battering the car ferociously, reminding her as nothing else could just how perilous their situation was. Gripping the wheel tighter, her heart pounding, she pressed the accelerator again more cautiously and drove on, almost blinded by the blizzard.

Before she'd gone more than a few feet she hit a drift with her right front wheel, and her car slewed round and came to rest across the road, wedged up against the bank behind her. After a few moments of spinning the wheels fruitlessly, she slammed her hand on the steering wheel and stifled a scream of frustration tinged with panic.

'Mummy?'

'It's OK, darling. We're just a teeny bit stuck. I need to have a look outside. I won't be long.'

She tried to open her door, but it wouldn't budge, and she wound the window down and peered out into the blizzard, shielding her eyes from the biting sting of the snow crystals that felt as if they were coming straight from the Arctic.

She was up against a snowdrift, rammed tight into it, and there was no way she'd be able to open the door. She shut the window fast and shook the snow out of her hair.

'Wow! That was a bit blowy!' she said with a grin over her shoulder, but Josh wasn't reassured.

'Don't like it, Mummy,' he said, his lip wobbling ominously.

Nor do I. And I don't need them walking in a winter wonderland on the radio!

'It's fine, Josh. It's just snowing a bit fast at the

moment, but it won't last. I'll just get out of the other door and see why we're stuck.'

'No! Mummy stay!'

'Darling, I'll be just outside. I'm not going away.'

'P'omise?'

'I promise.'

She blew him a kiss, scrambled across to the passenger side and fought her way out into the teeth of the blizzard to assess the situation. Difficult, with the biting wind lashing her hair across her eyes and finding its way through her clothes into her very bones, but she checked first one end of the car, then the other, and her heart sank.

It was firmly wedged, jammed between the snowdrift she'd run into on the right and the snow that had fallen down behind them, probably dislodged as she'd slid sideways. The car had embedded itself firmly against the right bank, and there was nothing she could do. She could never dig it out alone with her bare hands, not with the snow drifting so rapidly off the field in the howling wind. It was already a few inches deep. Soon the exhaust pipe would be covered, and the engine would stall, and they'd die of cold.

Literally.

Their only hope, she realised as she shielded her eyes from the snow again and assessed the situation, lay in the house behind those beautiful but intimidating gates.

Easton Court. The home of Sebastian Corder, the man she'd loved with all her heart, the man she'd left because he'd been chasing something she couldn't understand or identify with at the expense of their relationship.

He'd expected her to drop everything and follow him into a lifestyle she hated, abandoning her career, her family, even her principles, and when she'd asked him to reconsider, he'd refused and so she'd walked away, leaving her heart behind...

And now her life and the life of her child might depend on him.

This house, the house she'd fallen so in love with, home of the only man she'd ever really loved, was the last place in the world she wanted to be, its owner the last man in the world she wanted to ask for help. She didn't imagine he'd be any more thrilled than she was, but she had Josh with her, and so she had no choice but to swallow her pride and hope to God he was there.

Heart pounding, she struggled to the gate, lifted a hand so cold she could scarcely feel it and scrubbed the snow away from the intercom with her icy fingers.

'Please be there,' she whispered, 'please help me.' And then, her heart in her mouth, she pressed the button and waited.

The sharp, persistent buzz cut through his concentration, and he stopped what he was doing, pressed save and headed for the hall.

This would be the last of his Christmas deliveries. Hurray for online shopping, he thought, and then glanced out of the window and did a mild double-take. When had it started snowing like that?

He looked at the screen on the intercom and frowned. He couldn't see anything for a moment, just a swirl of white, and then the screen cleared momentarily and he made out the figure of a woman, huddled up in her coat, her hands tucked under her arms—and then she pulled a hand out and swiped snow off the front of the intercom and he saw her clearly.

Georgie?

He felt the blood drain from his head and hauled in a breath, then another one. No. It couldn't be. He was seeing things, conjuring her up out of nowhere because he couldn't stop thinking about her while he was in this damn house—

'Can I help you?' he said crisply, not trusting his eyes, but then she swiped the hair back off her face and anchored it out of the way, and it really was her, her smile tentative but relieved as she heard his voice.

'Oh, Sebastian, thank goodness you're there. I wasn't sure—um—it's Georgie Pullman. Georgia Becket? Look, I'm really sorry to trouble you, but can you help me? I wouldn't ask, but my car's stuck in a snowdrift just by your gateway, and I don't have a spade to dig myself out and my phone won't work.'

He hesitated, holding his breath and staring at her while he groped frantically for a level surface in a world that suddenly seemed tilted on its axis. And then it righted and common sense prevailed. Sort of.

'Wait there. I'll drive down. Maybe I can tow you out.'

'Thanks. You're a star.'

She vanished in a swirl of whiteout, and he let go of the button with a sharp sigh. What the hell was she doing driving along the lane in this weather?

Surely not coming to see him? Why would she? She never had, not once in nine years, and he had no reason to think she'd do it now—unless it was curiosity about the house, and he doubted it. Not in this weather, and probably not at all. Why would she care? She hadn't cared enough to stay with him.

She'd hated him in the end, and he couldn't blame her. He'd hated himself, but he'd hated her, too, for what she'd done to them, for not having faith in him, for not sticking by him just when he'd needed her the most.

No, she wasn't coming to see him. She'd been going home to her parents for Christmas, using the short cut, and now here she was, purely by chance, stuck outside his house and he had no choice— no damn choice at all—but to go and dig her out. And that would mean talking to her, seeing her face, hearing her voice.

Resurrecting a whole shed-load of memories of a time he'd rather forget.

Dragging that up all over again was the last thing he needed, but just moving here had done that, anyway, and there was no way he could leave her outside in a blizzard. And it'd be dark soon. The light was failing already. He'd dig her out and send her on her way. Fast, before it was too late and he was stuck with her.

Letting out a low growl, he picked up his car keys, shrugged on his coat, grabbed a shovel and a tow rope from the coach-house and threw them into the back of the Range Rover he'd bought for just this sort of eventuality. Not that he'd ever expected to be digging Georgia out of a hole.

He headed down the drive, his wipers going flat

out to clear the screen, but when he got to the gates and opened them with the remote control, there was no sign of her. Just footprints in the deep snow, heading to the left and vanishing fast in the blizzard.

It was far worse than he'd realised. There were no huge, fat flakes that drifted softly down and stayed where they fell, but tiny crystals of snow driven horizontally by the biting wind, the drifts piling up and making the lane impassable. He wondered where the hell she was. It would have been handy to know just how far along—

And then he saw it, literally yards from the end of his drive, the red tail lights dim through the coating of snow over the lenses. He left the car in the gateway and got out, his boots sinking deep into the powdery drifts as he crunched towards her. No wonder she was stuck, going out in weather like this in that ridiculous little car, but there was no way she'd be going anywhere else in it tonight, he realised. Which meant he *would* be stuck with her.

Damn.

He felt anger moving in, taking the place of shock. Good. Healthy. Better than the sentimental wallowing he'd been doing last night in that damn four-poster bed—

Bracing himself against the wind, he turned his collar up against the needles of ice and strode over to it, opening the passenger door and stooping down. A blast of warmth and Christmas music swamped him, and carried on the warmth was a lingering scent that he remembered so painfully, excruciatingly well.

It hit him like a kick in the gut, and he slammed the lid on his memories and peered inside.

She was kneeling on the seat looking at something in the back, and as she turned towards him she gave him a tentative smile.

'Hi. That was quick. I'm really sorry—'

'Don't worry about it,' he said crisply, trying not to scan her face for changes. 'Right, let's get you out of here.'

'See, Josh?' she said cheerfully. 'I told you he was going to help us.'

Josh? She had a *Josh* who could dig her out?

'Josh?' he said coldly, and her smile softened, stabbing him in the gut.

'My son.'

She had a son?

His heart pounding, he ducked his head in so he could look over the back of the seat—and met wide eyes so familiar they seemed to cut right to his soul.

'Josh, this is Sebastian. He's going to get us unstuck.'

He was? Well, of course he was! How could he refuse those liquid green eyes so filled with uncertainty? Poor little kid.

'Hi, Josh,' he said softly, because after all it wasn't the child's fault they were stuck, and then he finally let himself look at Georgie.

She hadn't changed at all. She had the same wide, ingenuous eyes as her son, the same soft bow lips, high cheekbones and sweeping brows that had first enchanted him all those years ago. Her wild curls were dark and glossy and beaded with melted snow, and there was a tiny pleat of worry between her brows. And her face was just inches from his, her scent swirling around him in the shelter of the car and making mincemeat of his carefully erected defences.

He hauled his head out of the car and straightened up, sucking in a lungful of freezing air. Better. Slightly. Now if he could just nail those defences back in place again—

'I'm really sorry,' she began again, peering up at him, but he shook his head.

'Don't. Let's just get your car out of here and get you inside.'

'No! I need to get to my parents!'

He let his breath out on a disbelieving huff. 'Georgie, look at it!' he said, gesturing at the weather. 'You're going nowhere. I don't even know if I can get your car out, and you're certainly not taking it anywhere else in the dark.'

'It's not dark—'

'Almost. And we haven't got your car out yet. Just get in the driver's seat, keep the engine running and when you feel a tug let the brakes off and reverse gently back as I pull you. And try and steer it so it doesn't go in the ditch. OK?'

She opened her mouth, shut it again and nodded.

Plenty of time once the car was out to argue with him.

It took just moments.

The car slithered and slid, and for a second she thought they'd end up in the ditch, but then she felt the tug from behind ease off as they came to rest outside the gates and she put the handbrake on and relaxed her grip on the wheel.

Phase 1 over. Now for Phase 2.

She opened the car door and got out into the blizzard again. He was right there, checking the side of her car that had been wedged against the snowdrift, and he straightened and met her eyes.

'It looks OK. I don't think it's damaged.'

'Good. That's a relief. And thanks for helping me—'

'Don't thank me,' he said bluntly. 'You were blocking the lane, I've only cleared it before the snow plough comes along and mashes it to a pulp.'

She gulped down the snippy retort. Of course he wasn't going to be gracious about it! She was the last person he wanted to turn out to help, but he'd done it anyway, so she swallowed her pride and tried again. 'Well, whatever, I'm still grateful. I'll be on my way now—'

He cut her off with a sharp sigh. 'We've just had this conversation, Georgia. You can't go anywhere. Your car won't get down the lane. Nothing will. I could hardly pull you out with the Range Rover. What on earth possessed you to try and drive down here in weather like this anyway?'

She blinked and stared at him. 'I had to. I'm on my way home to my parents for Christmas, and I thought I'd beat the snow, but it came out of nowhere and for the last hour I've just been crawling along—'

'So why come this way? It's hardly the most sensible route in that little tin can.'

She bristled. Tin can? 'I wasn't coming this way but the other road was closed with an accident— d'you know what? Forget it!' she snapped, losing her temper completely because absolutely the last place in the world she wanted to be snowed in was with this bad-tempered and ungracious reminder of the worst time of her life, and she was seriously leaving now! *In her tin can!* 'I'm really sorry I disturbed you, I'll make sure I never do it again. Just—just go back to your ivory tower and leave me alone and I'll get out of your hair!'

She tried to get back in the car, desperate to get away before the weather got any worse, but his hand shot out and clamped round her wrist like a vice.

'Georgia, grow up! No matter how tempted I am to leave you here to work it out for yourself—and believe me, I am *very* tempted at the moment—I can't let you both die of your stubborn, stiff-necked stupidity.'

Her eyes widened and she glared at him, trying to wrestle her arm free. 'Stubborn, stiff-necked—? Well, you can talk! You're a past master at that! And we're not going to die. You're being ridiculously melodramatic. It's simply not that bad.'

It was his turn to snap then, his temper flayed by that intoxicating scent and the deluge of memories that apparently just wouldn't be stopped. He tugged her closer, glowering down into her face as the scent assailed him once more.

'Are you sure?' he growled. 'Because I can leave you here to test the theory, if you insist, but I am *not* leaving your son in the car with you while you do it.'

'You can't touch him—'

'Watch me,' he said flatly. 'He's—what? Two? Three?'

The fight went out of her eyes, replaced by maternal worry. 'Two. He's two.'

He closed his eyes fleetingly and swallowed the wave of nausea. He'd been two…

'Right,' he said, his voice tight but reasoned now, 'I'm going to unhitch my car, drive into the entrance and hitch yours up again and pull you up the drive—'

'No. Just leave me here,' she pleaded. 'We'll be all right. The accident will be cleared by now. I'll turn round and go back the other way—'

His mouth flattened into a straight, implacable line. 'No. Believe me, I don't want this any more than you do, but unlike you I take my responsibilities seriously—'

'How dare you!' she yelled, because that was just the last straw. 'I take my responsibilities seriously! *Nothing* is more important to me than Josh!'

'Then prove it! Get in the car, shut up and do as you're told just for *once* in your life before we all freeze to death—and turn that blasted radio off!'

He dropped her arm like a hot brick, and she got back in the car, slammed the door unnecessarily hard and a shower of snow slid off the roof and blocked the wipers.

'Mummy?'

Oh, Josh.

'It's OK, darling.' Hell, her voice was shaking. She was shaking all over—

'Don't like him. Why he cross?'

'He's just cross with the snow, Josh, like Mummy. It's OK.'

A gloved hand swiped across the screen and the wipers started moving again, clearing it just enough that she could see his car in front of her now, pointing into the gateway. He was bending over, looking for the towing eye, probably, and seconds later he was dropping a loop over the tow hitch on his car and easing away from her.

She felt the tug, then the car slithered round and followed him obediently while she quietly seethed. Behind them she could see the gates begin to close, trapping her inside, and in front of them lights glowed dimly in the gloom.

Easton Court, home of her broken dreams.

Her prison for the next however long?

She should have just sat it out in the traffic jam.

CHAPTER TWO

HE TOWED HER all the way up the drive and round into the old stable yard behind the house, and by the time he pulled up he'd got his temper back under control.

Not so the memories, but if he could just keep his mouth shut he might not say anything he'd regret.

Anything *else* he'd regret. Too late for what he'd already said today, and far too late for all the words they'd said nine years ago, the bitterness and acrimony and destruction they'd brought down on their relationship.

All this time later, he still couldn't see who'd been right or wrong, or even if there'd been a right or wrong at all. He just knew he missed her, he'd never stopped missing her, and all he'd done about it in those intervening years was to ignore it, shut it away in a cupboard marked 'No Entry'.

And she'd just ripped the door right off it. She and this damned house. Well, that would teach him to give in to sentiment. He should have let it rot and then he wouldn't have been here.

So who would have rescued them? No-one?

He sucked in a deep breath, got out of the car and detached the tow rope, flinging it back into the car on top of the shovel just in case there were any other lunatics out on the lane today, although he doubted it. He could hardly see his hand in front of his face for the snow now, and that was in the shelter of the stable yard.

Dammit, if this didn't let up soon he was going to be stuck with her for days, her and her two-year-old son, with fathoms-deep eyes that could break your heart. And that, more than anything, was what was getting to him. The child, and what might have happened to him if he'd not been there to help—

'Oh, man up, Corder,' he growled to himself, and slammed the tailgate.

* * *

'OK, little guy?'

She turned and looked at Josh over her shoulder, his face all eyes and doubt.

'Want G'annie and G'anpa.'

'I know, but we can't get there today because of the snow, so we're going to stay here tonight with Sebastian in his lovely house and have an adventure!'

She tried to smile, but it felt so false. She was dreading going inside with Sebastian into the house that contained so much of their past. It would trash all her happy memories, and the tense, awkward atmosphere, the unspoken recriminations, the hurt and pain and regret lurking just under the surface of her emotions would make this so difficult to cope with, but it wasn't his fault she was here and the least she could do was be a little gracious and accept his grudging hospitality.

She glanced round as her nemesis walked over to her car and opened the door.

'I'm sorry.'

They said it in unison, and he gave her a crooked

smile that tore at her heart and stood back to let her out.

'Let's get you both in out of this. Can I give you a hand with anything?'

'Luggage? Realistically I'm not going anywhere tonight, am I?' She said it with a wry smile, and he let out a soft huff of laughter and started to pick up the luggage she was pulling from the boot.

He wondered how much one woman and a very small boy could possibly need for a single night. Baby stuff, he guessed, and slung a soft bag over his shoulder as he picked up another case and a long rectangular object she said was a travel cot.

'That should do for now. I might need to come back for something later.'

'OK.' He shut the tailgate as she opened the back door and reached in, emerging moments later with Josh.

Her son, he thought, and was shocked at the surge of jealousy at the thought of her carrying another man's child.

The grapevine had failed him, because he hadn't known she'd had a baby, but he'd known that her husband had died. A while ago now—a year, maybe two. While she was pregnant? The jealousy ebbed away, replaced by compassion. God, that must have been tough. Tough for all of them.

The boy looked at him solemnly for a moment with those huge, wary eyes that bored right through to his soul and found him wanting, and Sebastian turned away, swallowing a sudden lump in his throat, and led them in out of the cold.

'Oh!'

She stopped dead in the doorway and stared around her, her jaw sagging. He'd brought her into the oldest part of the house, through a lobby that acted as a boot room and into a warm and welcoming kitchen that could have stepped straight out of the pages of a glossy magazine.

His smile was wry. 'It's a bit different, isn't it?' he offered, and she gave a slight, disbelieving laugh.

The last time she'd seen it, it had been dark, gloomy and had birds nesting in it.

Not any more. Now, it was…

'Just a bit,' she said weakly. 'Wow.'

He watched her as she looked round the kitchen, her lips parted, her eyes wide. She was taking in every detail of the transformation, and he assessed her reaction, despising himself for caring what she thought and yet somehow, in some deep, dark place inside himself that he didn't want to analyse, needing her approval.

Ridiculous. He didn't need her approval for anything in his life. She'd given up the right to ask for that on the day she'd walked out, and he wasn't giving it back to her now, tacitly or otherwise.

He shrugged off his coat and hung it over the back of a chair by the Aga, then picked up the kettle.

'Tea?'

She dragged her eyes away from her cataloguing of the changes to the house and looked at him warily, nibbling her lip with even white teeth until he found himself longing to kiss away the tiny indentations she was leaving in its soft, pink plumpness—

'If you don't mind.'

But they'd already established that he did mind, in that tempestuous and savage exchange outside the gate, and he gave an uneven sigh and rammed a hand through his hair. It was wet with snow, dripping down his neck, and hers must be, too. Hating himself for that loss of temper and control, he got a tea towel out of the drawer and handed it to her, taking another one for himself.

'Here,' he said gruffly. 'Your hair's wet. Go and stand by the Aga and warm up.'

It wasn't an apology, but it could have been an olive branch and she accepted it as that. They were stuck with each other, there was nothing either of them could do about it, and Josh was cold and scared and hungry. And the snow was dripping off her hair and running down her face.

She propped herself up on the front of the Aga, Josh on her hip, and towelled her hair with her free hand while she tried not to study him. 'Tea would be lovely, please, and if you've got one Josh would probably like a biscuit.'

'No problem. I think we could probably withstand a siege—my entire family are here for

Christmas from tomorrow so the cupboards are groaning. It's my first Christmas in the house and I offered to host it for my sins.'

'I expect they're looking forward to it. Your parents must be glad to have you close again.'

He gave a slightly bitter smile and turned away, giving her a perfect view of his broad shoulders as he got mugs out of a cupboard. 'Needs must. My mother's not well. She had a heart attack three years ago, and they gave her a by-pass at Easter.'

Ouch. She'd loved his mother, but his relationship with her had been a little rocky, although she'd never really been able to work out why. 'I'm sorry to hear that. I didn't know. I hope she's OK now.'

'She's getting over it—and why would you know? Unless you're keeping tabs on my family as well as me?' he said, his voice deceptively mild as he turned to look at her with those penetrating dark eyes.

She stared at him, taken aback by that. 'I'm not keeping tabs on you!'

'But you knew I was living here. When I answered the intercom, you knew it was me. There was no hesitation.'

As if she wouldn't have known his voice anywhere, she thought with a dull ache in her chest.

'I didn't know you'd moved in,' she told him honestly. 'That was just sheer luck under the circumstances, but the fact that you'd bought it was hardly a state secret. You were rescuing a listed house of historical importance on the verge of ruin, and people were talking about it. Bear in mind my husband was an estate agent.'

He frowned. That made sense. He contemplated saying something, but what? Sorry he'd died? Bit late to offer his condolences, and he hadn't felt able to at the time. Because it felt inappropriate? Probably. Or just keeping his distance from her, desperately trying to keep her in that cupboard she'd just ripped the door off. And now, in front of the child, wasn't the time to initiate that conversation.

So, after a pause in which he filled the kettle, he brought the subject back to the house. Safer, marginally, so long as he kept his memories under control.

'I didn't realise it had caused such a stir,' he said casually.

'Well, of course it did. It was on the at-risk register for years. I think everyone expected it to fall down before it was sold.'

'It wasn't that close. There wasn't much wrong with it that money couldn't solve, but the owner couldn't afford to do anything other than repair the roof and he hadn't wanted to sell it for development, so before he died he put a restrictive covenant on it to say it couldn't be divided or turned into a hotel. And apparently nobody wants a house like this any more. Too costly to repair, too costly to run, too much red tape because of the listing— it goes on and on, and so it just sat here waiting while the executors tried to get the covenant lifted.'

'And then you rescued it.'

Because he hadn't been able to forget it. Or her.

'Yeah, well, we all make mistakes sometimes,' he muttered, and lifting the hob cover, he put the kettle on, getting another drift of her scent as he did so. He moved away, making a production of finding biscuits for Josh as he opened one cupboard after another, and she watched him thoughtfully.

We all make mistakes sometimes.

Really? He thought it was a mistake? Why? Because it had been a money-sink? Or because of all the memories—memories that were haunting her even now, standing here with him in the house where they'd fallen in love?

'Well, mistake or not,' she said softly, 'I'm really glad you're here, because otherwise we'd still be out there in the snow and it's not letting up. And you're right,' she acknowledged. 'It could have ended quite differently.'

He met her eyes then, his brows tugging briefly together in a frown. He'd only been back here a couple of days. And if he'd still been away—

'Yes. It could. Look, we'll see how it is tomorrow. If the wind drops and the snow eases off, I might be able to get you to your parents in the

Range Rover, even if you can't get your car there for now.'

She nodded. 'Thank you. That would be great. And I really am sorry. I know I was a stroppy cow out there, but I was just scared and I wanted to get home.'

His mouth flickered in a brief smile. 'Don't worry about it. So—I take it you approve of what I've done in here?' he asked to change the subject, and then wanted to kick himself. Finally engaging his brain on the task of finding some biscuits, he opened the door of the pantry cupboard and stared at the shelves while he had another go at himself for fishing for her approval.

'Well, I do so far,' she said to his back. 'If this is representative of the rest of the house, you've done a lovely job of rescuing it.'

'Thanks.' He just stopped himself from offering her a guided tour, and grabbed a packet of amaretti biscuits and turned towards her. 'Are these OK?' he asked, and she nodded.

'Lovely. Thank you. He really likes those.'

Josh pointed at them and squirmed to get down.

'Biscuit,' he said, eyeing Sebastian as if he didn't quite trust him.

'Say please,' she prompted.

'P'ees.'

She put him on the floor and took off his coat, tugging the cuffs as he pulled his arms out, but then instead of coming over to get a biscuit from him, he stood there next to her, one arm round her leg, watching Sebastian with those wary eyes.

He opened the packet, then held it out.

'Here. Take them to Mummy, see if she wants one.'

He hesitated for a second then let go of her leg and took the packet, eyes wide, and ran back to her, tripping as he got there and scattering a few on the floor.

'Oops—three second rule,' she said with a grin that kicked him in the chest, and knelt down and gathered them up.

'Here,' he said, offering her a plate, and she put them on it and stood up with a rueful smile, just inches from him.

'Sorry about that.'

He backed away to a safe distance. 'Don't worry about it. It was my fault, I didn't think. He's only little.'

'Oh, he can do it. He's just a bit overawed by it all.'

And on the verge of tears now, hiding his face in his mother's legs and looking uncertain.

'Hey, I reckon we'd better eat these up, don't you, Josh?' Sebastian said encouragingly, and he took one of the slightly chipped biscuits from the plate, then glanced at Georgia. 'In case you're wondering, the floor's pristine. It was washed this morning.'

'No pets?'

He shook his head. 'No pets.'

'I thought a dog by the fire was part of the dream?' she said lightly, and then could have kicked herself, because his face shut down and he turned away.

'I gave up dreaming nine years ago,' he said flatly, and she let out a quiet sigh and gave Josh a biscuit.

'Sorry. Forget I said that. I'm on autopilot. In

fact, do you think I could borrow your landline? I should call my mother—but I can't get a signal. She'll be wondering where we are.'

'Sure. There's one there.'

She nodded, picked it up and turned away, and he glanced down at the child.

Their eyes met, and Josh studied him briefly before pointing at the biscuits. 'More biscuit. And d'ink, Mummy.'

Georgia found a feeder cup and gave it to him to give Sebastian. 'What do you say?' she prompted from the other side of the kitchen.

'P'ees.'

'Good boy.' Sebastian smiled at him as he took the cup, and the child smiled back shyly, making his heart squeeze.

Poor little tyke. He'd been expecting to go to his loving and welcoming grandparents, and he'd ended up with a grumpy recluse with a serious case of the sulks. Good job, Corder.

'Here, let's sit down,' he said, and sat on the floor, handed Josh his plastic feeder cup, and they tucked into the biscuits while he tried not to eavesdrop on Georgie's conversation.

She glanced over her shoulder, and saw Josh was on the floor with Sebastian. They seemed to be demolishing the entire plateful of biscuits, and she hid a smile.

He'd never eat all his supper, but frankly she didn't care. The fact that Josh wasn't still clinging to her leg was a minor miracle, and she let them get on with it while she soothed her mother.

'Mum, we're fine. The person who lives here is taking very good care of us, and he's been very kind and got my car off the road, so we're warm and safe and it's all good.'

'Are you sure? Because you can't be too careful.'

'Absolutely. It's just for tonight, and it'll be clear by tomorrow. They've got a Range Rover so he's going to give us a lift,' she said optimistically, crossing her fingers.

'Oh, well, that's all right, then,' her mother said with relief in her voice. 'I'm glad you're both safe, we were worried sick when you didn't ring, so do keep in touch. We'll see you tomorrow, and you stay safe. And give my love to Josh.'

'Will do. Bye, Mum.'

She cut the connection and put the phone back on the charger, then turned and met his eyes. A brow flickered eloquently.

'They?' he murmured.

'Figure of speech.' And less of a red flag to her mother than 'he'…

He humphed slightly. 'You didn't tell her where you are.'

She blinked. 'Why would I?'

The brow flickered again. 'Lying by omission?'

She shrugged off her coat and draped it over a chair next to his at the huge table. 'It's not a lie, it's just an unnecessary fact that changes nothing material. And what she doesn't know…'

He didn't answer, just held her eyes for an endless moment before turning away. The kettle had boiled and he was making tea now while Josh cleaned up the last few crumbs on the plate, and she picked it up before he could break it.

'Here—your tea.' Sebastian put her cup down

in the middle of the table out of Josh's reach and picked up his coat.

'Give me your keys. I'll put your car away in the coach-house. Is there anything else you need out of it?'

'Oh. There's a bag of Christmas presents. There are some things in there that don't really need to freeze. It's in the boot.'

'OK.' She passed him the keys and he went out, and she let the breath ease out of her lungs.

Just one night, she told herself. *You can do this. And at least you know he's not an axe murderer, so it could have been worse.*

'Mummy, finished.'

Josh handed her his cup and she found him a book in the changing bag and sat him on her lap. She was reading to him when Sebastian came back in a few minutes later, stamping snow off his boots and brushing it off his head and shoulders.

She put her tea down and stared at him in dismay. 'No sign of it stopping, then?'

He shook his head and held out her keys, and she reached out to take them, her fingers closing round his for a moment. They were freezing cold, wet with the snow, and she shivered slightly with the thought of what might have been. If he hadn't been here…

'Sebastian—thank you. For everything.'

His eyes searched hers, then flicked away. 'You're welcome.' He shrugged off his coat and hung it up again. 'I'll go and make sure your room's ready.'

'You don't need to do that just for one night! I can sleep on a sofa—'

He stared at her as if she'd sprouted another head. 'It's a ten-bedroomed house! Why on earth would you want to do that?'

'I just don't want you to go to any more trouble.'

'It's no trouble, the rooms are already made up. Where do you want these?'

'Ah.' She eyed the presents. 'Can you find somewhere for them that's not my room? Just to be on the safe side.'

'Sure. If you need the cloakroom it's at the end of the hall.'

He picked up all her bags and went out, and she

let out her breath on another sigh. She hadn't realised she'd been holding it again, and the slackening of tension when he left the room was a huge relief.

She felt a tug on her sweater. 'Mummy, more biscuit.'

'No, Josh. You can't have any more. You won't eat your supper.'

'Supper at G'annie's house?' he said hopefully, and she shook her head, watching his face fall.

'No, darling, we're staying here. Grannie sends you her love and a great big kiss and she'll see you tomorrow, if it's stopped snowing.' Which it had better have done soon. She scooped him up and kissed him.

'I tell you what, why don't we play hide and seek?' she suggested, trying to inject some excitement into her voice, and he giggled and squirmed down. As she counted to ten he disappeared under the table, his little rump sticking out between the chair legs.

'I hiding! Mummy find me!'

'Oh! Where's he gone? Josh? Jo-osh, where are

you?' she called softly, in a sing-song voice, and pretended to look. She opened the door Sebastian had got the biscuits from, and found a pantry cupboard laden with goodies. Heavens, he was right, they were ready for a siege! The shelves were groaning with expensive food from exclusive London shops like Fortnum's and Harrods, and the contents of the pantry were probably equal to her annual food budget.

She shut the door quickly and went back to her 'search' for the giggling child. 'Jo-osh! Where are you?'

She opened another cupboard, and found an enormous built-in fridge, then behind the next door a huge crockery cupboard. It was an exquisitely made hand-built painted kitchen, every piece custom made of solid wood and beautifully constructed, finished in a muted grey eggshell that went perfectly with the cream walls and the black slate floor. And rather than granite, the worktops were made of oiled wood—more traditional, softer than granite, warmer somehow.

The whole effect was classy and elegant at the

same time as being homely and welcoming, and it was also well designed, an efficient working triangle. He'd done it properly—or someone had—

'Mummy! I here!'

'Josh? Goodness, I'm sure I can hear you, but I can't see you anywhere!'

'I under the table!'

'Under the table?'

She knelt down and peered through the legs of the chairs, bottom in the air, and of course that was how Sebastian found her when he came in a second later.

'Georgie?'

She closed her eyes briefly. *Marvellous*. She lifted her head and swiped her hair back out of her eyes as she sat back on her heels, her dignity in tatters. She could feel her cheeks flaming, and she swallowed hard. 'Hi,' she said, trying to smile. 'We're playing hide and seek.'

He gave a soft, rueful laugh. 'Nothing much changes, does it?' he murmured, and she felt heat sweep over her body.

They'd played hide and seek in the house often

after that first time, and every time he'd found her, he'd kissed her.

She remembered it vividly, so vividly, and she could feel her cheeks burning up.

'Apparently not,' she said, and got hastily to her feet, brushing the non-existent dust from her jeans, ridiculously flustered. 'Um—I could probably do with changing his nappy. Where did you put our bags?'

'In your room. It's the one at the end of the landing on the right—do you want me to show you?'

'That might be an idea.'

Not because she needed showing, but because she didn't want to be tempted to stray into his room. He would have the master suite in the middle at the front, overlooking the carriage sweep, and the stairs came up right beside it.

Too tempting.

She called Josh, took his hand in hers and followed Sebastian up the elegant Georgian staircase and resolutely past the slightly open door of the bedroom where she'd given him her body—and her heart…

* * *

Why on earth had he brought up the past when she'd mentioned hide and seek?

Idiot, he chided himself. He'd already had to leave the kitchen on the pretext of putting the cars away when she'd taken her coat off and he'd seen the lush, feminine curves that motherhood had given her.

She'd always had curves, but they were rounder now, softer somehow, utterly unlike the scrawny beanpoles he normally came into contact with, and he ached to touch her, to mould the soft fullness, to cradle the smooth swell of her bottom in his hand and ease her closer.

Much closer.

So much closer that he'd had to get out of the kitchen and give himself a moment.

Now he realised it was going to take a miracle, not a moment, because when he'd run out of things to do he'd walked back in to the sight of that rounded bottom sticking up into the air as she played under the table with the baby, and then she'd straightened, her cheeks still pink from bending over, and he'd seen straight down the V neck of her sweater to the enticing valley between those soft, rounded breasts and lust had hit him like a sledgehammer.

'Here,' he said, pushing open the door of her room. 'It's got its own bathroom, but I haven't put up the travel cot, I'm afraid. I wouldn't know where to start—is that OK? Can you manage?'

'Oh. Yes. That's fine. Um—I don't suppose you've got a small blanket—a fleecy one or something? And a sheet? I don't have any bedding with me because my mother keeps some at hers.'

'I'm sure I can find something. I'll see you in the kitchen when you're done,' he said, and left them to it.

She looked around at the lovely room, beautifully furnished with antiques, and wondered who'd sourced everything. Him? It seemed unlikely. He'd probably paid an interior designer an obscene amount of money to do it, but that was fine, he had it.

He'd been outrageously successful, by all accounts, made a killing on the stock market in the early days and re-invested the money in other businesses. He had a reputation for being fair but firm, and companies that he'd taken over had been turned around and sold for vast amounts, or retained in his portfolio to earn him a nice little income.

Not that she'd been keeping tabs on him…

She sighed. 'Come here, Josh. Let's do your nappy.'

But Josh was exploring, investigating the utterly decadent bathroom with its free-standing white-enamelled bateau bath, the vintage loo with ornate high level cistern and gleaming brass downpipe, the vintage china basin set on an old marble-topped washstand painted the same soft grey as the kitchen and the outside of the bath. There was a rack piled high with sumptuous, fluffy white towels, and expensive toiletries stood on the side of the washstand.

Gorgeous. Utterly, utterly gorgeous. She eyed the bath longingly. Maybe later.

'Come on, tinker. Let's change you.'

But he ran off, giggling, and she had to chase

him and catch him and pin him down, squirming like an eel and brimming with mischief. No wonder she didn't need the gym! Even if she had time, which she didn't. She hitched his trousers back up victoriously, mission accomplished, and grinned at him.

'Right, let's go back downstairs and have that tea, shall we?'

And see Sebastian again.

She bit her lip. He was being polite but distant, and she told herself it was what she wanted. Well, of course it was.

Except apparently her heart didn't think so, and a tiny corner of it was disappointed that he hadn't seemed pleased to see her. Well, what had she expected? She'd dumped him because he was too ambitious, too driven, too different from the boy she'd fallen in love with four years earlier, and he hadn't even tried to understand how she'd felt.

She obviously hadn't been that important to him then, and she certainly wouldn't be now, toting another man's child.

She rounded Josh up, took his hand and led him

towards the stairs, but then he slipped out of her grasp and ran through a doorway.

The doorway to the master bedroom, she realised, and her heart sank.

'Josh? Come out. That's not our room.'

Silence.

Which left her no choice but to go in...

She pushed the door open and looked around, and the first thing she saw was the bed, huge, beautiful, piled high with snowy white linen and taking her breath away. To be fair, it would have been hard to miss even in such a large room, but it dominated the space, leaping out of her fantasies and taunting her with its perfection, and she felt her cheeks burn.

She dragged her eyes away from it and looked around.

There was no sign of Josh—but the cupboard was there in the corner, the cupboard where she'd hidden, where Sebastian had found her and kissed her the first time.

And there, in front of the fireplace, was where he'd spread the blanket covered in petals and—

'Mummy, find me!'

She pressed a hand to her chest and sucked in a slow, steadying breath. What on earth was she *doing*? Why was she there? She shouldn't be here, in this room, in this house, with this man!

With her memories running riot—

'Mummy!'

She let out her breath, drew it in again and pinned a smile on her face, because he could always tell if she was smiling.

'Ready or not, here I come,' she sang, and heard the words echo down the years, ringing in the empty corridors as she'd hidden in the cupboard and held back her innocent, girlish laughter.

And then he'd kissed her and everything had changed...

CHAPTER THREE

THEY WERE TAKING ages.

Maybe she'd decided to unpack, or bath Josh, or perhaps she was lost.

He gave a soft snort. As if. She knew the house like the back of her hand. More likely she was exploring, giving herself a guided tour. She'd always considered the house to be her own private property. The concept of trespass never seemed to occur to her.

He went to look for her, taking the soft woollen throw he'd found for Josh's bed, and saw his bedroom door standing wide open and voices coming from inside.

'Josh, now! Come out from under there this minute or I'm going downstairs without you.'

Irritated, he walked in and was greeted yet again by that delectable bottom sticking up in the air.

Was she doing it on purpose? He dragged his eyes off it. 'Problems?' he asked crisply.

She jerked upright, her hand on her heart, and gave a little gasp. 'Oh—you startled me. I'm *so* sorry. The door was open and he ran in here and he's hiding under the middle of the bed and I can't reach him.'

She sounded exasperated and embarrassed, and he gave her the benefit of the doubt.

'Two-pronged attack?' he suggested with a slightly strained smile, and went round to the other side of the bed and lay down. 'Hello, Josh. Time to come out, little man.'

Josh shook his head and wriggled towards the other side, and then shrieked and giggled as his mother's hand closed over his arm and tugged gently.

'Come on, or you won't have supper.'

'Want biscuits.'

Sebastian opened his mouth to offer them and caught the warning look she shot him under the bed, and winked. 'No biscuits,' he said firmly.

'Not unless you come straight out and eat all your supper first.'

He was out in seconds, and Georgie scooped him up and plonked him firmly on her hip. She was smiling apologetically, her hair wildly tangled and out of control, those teeth catching her lip again, and he wanted her so much he could hardly breathe.

The air was full of tension, and he wondered if she was remembering that he'd kissed her here for the first time. They'd been playing hide and seek, and she'd hidden in the cupboard beside the chimney breast. He'd found her easily, just followed the sound of her muted laughter and hauled the door open to find her there, hand over her mouth to hold in the giggles, eyes so like Josh's brimming with mischief and something else, something much, much older than either of them, as old as time, and he'd followed her into the cupboard, cradled her face in his hands and kissed her.

He thought he'd died and gone to heaven.

'You kept the cupboard,' she said, her eyes flicking to it briefly, and he knew she was remembering it. Remembering, too, when he'd spread a picnic blanket on the middle of the bedroom floor and scattered it with the petals of the wisteria that still grew outside the bedroom window and laid her gently down—

'Yes. Well, it's useful,' he said gruffly, and dragged in some much-needed air. 'I put the kettle on because your tea was cold. It'll be boiling its head off.'

She seemed to draw herself back from the brink of something momentous, and her eyes flicked to his and away again, just as they had with the cupboard.

'Yes. Yes, it will. Come on, Josh, let's go and find you some supper.' She spun on her heel and walked swiftly out, the sound of her footsteps barely audible on the soft, thick carpet, and he didn't breathe until he heard her boot heels click hurriedly across the hall floor.

Then he let the air out in a rush and sat down heavily on the edge of the huge four-poster bed his interior designer had sourced for him without consultation and which haunted him every time he came in here. He sucked in another breath, but her scent was in the air and he closed his eyes, his hands fisting in the soft woollen throw, and struggled with a tidal wave of need and want and lust.

How was he going to survive this? The snow hadn't let up at all, and the forecast was atrocious. With that vicious wind blowing the snow straight off the field and dumping it in the lane, there was no way they'd be out of here in days, Range Rover or not. Nothing but a snow plough could get past three foot drifts, and that's what they'd been heading towards an hour ago.

Maybe the wind would drop overnight, he thought, but it was a vain hope. He could hear it now, rattling the windows in the front of the house, sweeping straight across from Siberia like a solid wall.

He swore under his breath, hauled in another lungful of air, straightened his shoulders and headed downstairs.

He'd keep out of her way. He could be polite but distant, give her the run of the kitchen and her bedroom and hide out in his study. Except he didn't want to, he discovered as he reached the hall and followed the sound of voices to the kitchen as if he'd been drawn by a magnet.

She turned with a wary smile as he walked in, and set a mug down on the table.

'I made you tea.'

'Thanks. What about Josh? What will he eat?'

'I don't know what you've got.'

He laughed softly and rolled his eyes. 'Everything. I gave my PA a guest list, a menu plan and a fairly loose brief. She used her initiative liberally.'

'I don't suppose she got any fish fingers?'

He felt himself recoil slightly. 'I doubt it. There's smoked salmon.'

She was suppressing a smile, and he could feel himself responding. 'So—shall I just look?' she suggested, and he nodded and gestured at the kitchen.

'Help yourself. Clearly I would have no idea where to start.'

He dropped into a chair and watched her and the child as she foraged in the cupboards and came up triumphant.

'Pasta and pesto with cherry tomatoes, Josh?'

Josh nodded and ran to a chair, trying to pull it out.

'I have to cook it, darling. Five minutes. Why don't you sit and read your book?'

But reading the book was boring, apparently, and he came over to Sebastian and leaned against his legs and looked up at him hopefully. 'Hide and seek?' he asked, and Sebastian stared at Georgie a trifle desperately because the very *last* thing he wanted to play was hide and seek, with his memories running riot—

'Won't he get lost?'

'In here? Hardly.'

'Just in here? There's nowhere to hide.'

'Oh, you'd be surprised,' she said, her laugh like music to his ears. 'Go and hide, Josh. Sebastian will count to ten and look for you.' She met his eyes over the table, mischief dancing in them. 'It's simple. He "hides",' she explained with little air quotes, 'and you look for him. I'm sure you can remember how it works.'

Oh, yes. He could remember how it all worked,

particularly the finding part. She'd never made that difficult after the first time...

He closed his eyes briefly, and when he opened them she'd looked away and was halving cherry tomatoes.

'Well, go on, then. Count!'

So he counted to ten, deluged with memories that refused to stay in their box, and then he got to his feet, ignoring the giggling child under the table, and said softly, 'Ready or not, here I come!'

Their eyes met, and he felt his heart bump against his ribs. The air seemed to be sucked out of the room, the tension palpable. And then she dropped the knife with a clatter, bent to pick it up and turned away, and he found he could breathe again.

'Has he settled?'

'Finally. I'm sorry it took so long.'

'Don't worry about it. It's a strange place. Will he be all right up there on his own?'

'Yes, he's gone out like a light now and I've got the baby monitor.'

He nodded. He was sprawled on a chair by the Aga, legs outstretched and crossed at the ankle, one arm resting on the dining table with a glass of wine held loosely in his fingers, watching the news.

He tilted his head towards the screen. 'The country seems to be gridlocked,' he said drily.

'Well, that's not a surprise. It always is if it snows.'

'Yeah. Well, there's over a foot already in the courtyard and the wind hasn't let up at all which doesn't bode well for the lane.'

'Which means you're stuck with us, then, doesn't it?' she said, her heart sinking, and swallowed. 'I'm so, so sorry. I should have left earlier, paid more attention to the weather forecast.' Gone the other way and stayed in the traffic jam, and she'd have been home by now instead of putting them both in this impossibly difficult situation.

He shook his head. 'They got it wrong. The wind picked up, a high pressure area shifted, and that was it. Not even you could cause this much havoc.'

But a wry smile softened his words, and he slid

the bottle towards her. 'Try this. It's quite interesting. I've found some duck breasts. I thought it
might go rather nicely.'

She poured a little into the clean glass that was
waiting, and sipped. 'Mmm. Lovely. So—do you
want me to cook for us?'

'No, I'll do it.'

She blinked. 'You can cook?'

'No,' he said drily. 'I have a resident house-
keeper and if she's got a day off I get something
delivered from the restaurant over the road—of
course I can cook! I've been looking after myself
for years. And anyway, my mother taught me.' He
uncrossed his legs and stood up. 'So—how does
pan-fried duck breast with a red wine and redcurrant *jus* on root-vegetable mash with tenderstem
broccoli and julienne carrots sound?'

'Like a restaurant menu,' she said, trying not to
laugh at him, but she had to bite her lips and he
balled up a tea towel and threw it at her, his lips
twitching.

'So is that yes or no?'

'Oh, yes—please. But only if you can manage it,' she added mischievously.

He rolled his eyes. 'Don't push your luck or you'll end up with beans on toast,' he warned, and rolled up his sleeves and started emptying the fridge onto the worktop.

'Can I help?'

'Yes. You can lay the table. I'll let you.'

'Big of you.'

'It is. Do it properly. The cutlery's in this drawer.'

She threw the tea towel back, catching him squarely in the middle of his chest, and he grabbed it and chuckled, and for a second the years seemed to melt away.

And then he turned, picking up a knife, and the moment was gone.

It was no hardship to watch him while he cooked.

She studied every nuance of his body, tracking the changes brought about in nine years. He'd only been twenty-one then, nearly twenty-two. Now, he was thirty-one, and a man in his prime.

Not that he'd been anything other than a man

then, there'd been no doubt about that, but now his shoulders under the soft cotton shirt seemed broader, more solidly muscled, and he seemed a little taller. The skilfully cut trousers hugged the same neat hips, though, and hinted at the taut muscles of his legs. She'd always loved his legs, and every time he shifted, her body tightened in response.

And while she watched, greedily drinking in every movement of the frame she'd once known so well, he peeled and chopped and sliced, mashed and seasoned, deglazed the frying pan with a sizzle of the lovely red, stirred in a hefty dollop of port and redcurrant sauce and then arranged it all with mathematical precision on perfectly warmed plates.

'Voilà!'

He set the plates down on the places she'd laid, and she smiled. 'Very pretty.'

'We aim to please. Dig in.'

She dug, her mouth watering, and it was every bit as good as it looked and smelled.

'Oh, wow,' she mumbled, and he gave a wry huff of laughter.

'See? No faith in me. You never have had.'

Georgie shook her head. 'I've always had faith in you. I always knew you'd be a success, and you are.'

Even if she hadn't been able to live with him any more.

He shrugged. There was success, and then there was happiness. That still eluded him, chased out by a restless, fretful search for his identity, his fundamental self, and it had cost him Georgia and everything that went with her. Everything she'd then had with another man—and he really didn't want to think about that. He changed the subject. Sort of.

'Josh seems a nice little kid. I didn't know you'd had a child.'

She met his eyes, her fork suspended in mid-air. 'Why would you unless you were keeping tabs on me?'

A smile touched his eyes. 'Touché,' he murmured softly, and the smile faded. 'I was sorry to hear about your husband. That must have been tough for you.'

Tough? He didn't know the half of it. 'It was,' she said quietly.

'What happened?'

She put her fork down. 'He had a heart attack. He was at work and I had a call to say he'd collapsed and died at his desk.'

He winced. 'Ouch. Wasn't he a bit young for that?'

'Thirty-nine. And we'd just moved and extended the mortgage, so things are a bit tight.'

'What about the life insurance? Surely that covered the mortgage?'

Her mouth twisted slightly. 'He'd cancelled it three months before.'

That shocked him. 'Cancelled it? Why would he cancel it?'

'Cash flow, I presume. Property wasn't selling, and because he'd cancelled the insurance of course they won't pay out, so I'm having to work full-time to pay the mortgage. And it's still not selling, so I can't shift the house, and I'm stuck.'

He rammed a hand through his hair. 'Oh, George. That's tough. I'm sorry.'

'Yeah, me, too, but there's nothing I can do. I just have to get on with it.'

He frowned, slowly turning his wine glass round and round by the stem with his thumb and forefinger. 'So what do you do with Josh while you're at work?'

'I have him with me. I work at home—mostly at night. He goes to nursery three mornings a week to give me a straight stretch of time, and it just about works.'

He topped up her glass and leaned back against the chair, his eyes searching her face. 'So what do you do?'

She smiled. 'I'm a virtual PA. My boss is very understanding, and we get by, but I won't pretend it's easy.'

'No, I'm sure it's not.' For either of them. He thought of how he'd manage if he and Tash weren't in the same office, and then realised that they weren't for a lot of the time, but that was because he was the one out of the office, not her, and she was there in the thick of it and able to get him answers at the touch of a button.

The other way round—well, the mind boggled.

'How old was Josh when it happened?'

'Two months.'

Sebastian felt sick. 'He won't remember him at all,' he said, his voice sounding hollow to his ears. 'That's such a shame.'

'It is, it's a real shame. David was so proud of him. He would have adored him.'

'You will tell Josh all about him, won't you?'

'Of course I will. And he's got grandparents, too. David's parents live in Cambridge. Don't worry. He'll know all about his father, Sebastian. I won't let him grow up in a vacuum.'

He felt the tension leave him, but a wave of grief followed it. He hadn't grown up in a vacuum, but he'd been living a lie and he hadn't known it until he was eighteen. And then this void had opened up, a yawning hole where once had been certainty, and nothing had been the same since. Especially not since he'd been privy to the finer details. Not that there was anything fine about them, by any stretch of the imagination.

Had his father been proud of him? Had his mother? Had her voice softened when she talked about her little son, the way Georgie's did?

Who was he?

Endless questions, but no proper answers, even after all this time, and realistically he knew now that there never would be. He sucked in a breath and turned his attention back to the food, but it tasted like sawdust.

'Hey—it's OK,' she said, frowning at him, her face concerned. 'We're doing all right. Life goes on.'

'Were you happy together, you and David?' he asked, wondering why he was beating himself up like this, but she didn't answer, and after a moment he looked up and met her eyes.

'He was a good man,' she said eventually. 'We lived in a nice house with good neighbours, we had some lovely friends—it was good.'

Good? What did that mean? Such an ineffectual

word—or maybe not. Good was more than he had. 'And did you love him?'

Her eyes went blank. 'I don't think that's any of your business,' she said softly, and put her cutlery down, the food unfinished.

'I'll take that as a no, then,' he said, pushing it because he was angry about Josh, angry that she'd been playing happy families with someone else while he'd been alone—

'Take it as whatever you like, Sebastian. As I said, it's none of your business. If you don't mind, I think I'll go to bed now.'

'And if I mind?'

She stood up and looked at him expressionlessly. 'Then I'm still going to bed. Thank you for my meal and your hospitality,' she said politely. 'I'll see you tomorrow.'

He watched her go, and he swore softly and dropped his head into his hands. Why? Why hadn't he kept his mouth shut? Getting angry with her wouldn't change anything, any more than it had nine years ago.

He was reaching for the wine bottle when the

lights on the baby monitor flashed, and he heard a sound that could have been a sigh or a sob or both.

'Why does he care, Josh? It's none of his business if I was happy with another man. *He* didn't make me happy in the long term, did he? He could have done, but he just didn't damn well care.'

Sebastian closed his eyes briefly, then picked up the baby monitor and took it upstairs, tapping lightly on her door and handing it to her silently when she opened it.

'Oh. Thanks.'

'You're welcome. And, for the record, I did care. I never stopped caring.'

She swallowed, and he could see the realisation that he'd heard everything she'd said register on her face. She coloured, but she didn't look away, just challenged him again, her voice soft so she didn't disturb the sleeping child.

'You didn't care enough to change for me, though, did you? You wouldn't even talk about it. You didn't even try to understand or explain why you never had time for me any more.'

No. He hadn't explained. He still couldn't. He wasn't sure he really knew himself, in some ways.

'I couldn't change,' he said, feeling exasperated and cornered. 'It wasn't possible. I had to do what I had to do to succeed, and I couldn't have changed that, not even for you.'

'No, Sebastian, you could have done. You just wouldn't.'

And she stepped back and closed the door quietly in his face.

He stared at the closed door, his thoughts reeling.

Was she right? Could he have changed the way he'd done things, made it easier for her to live the life he'd had to live?

Not really. Not without giving up all he'd worked for, all he'd done to try and find out who he really was, deep down under all the layers that had been superimposed by his upbringing.

He was still no closer to knowing the answer, and maybe he never would be, but until then he couldn't stop striving to find out, to explore every avenue, every facet of himself, to push himself to the limit until he found out where those limits were.

And on the way, he'd discovered he could make money. Serious money. Enough to make a difference to the people who mattered? Maybe. He hoped so. The charities he supported seemed to think he was making a difference to the kids.

But Georgie mattered, too, and she was right, there hadn't been time for her in all of this.

OK, it had been tough—tough for both of them. He'd had a hectic life—working all day, networking every evening in one way or another. Dinner out with someone influential. Private views. Trade fairs, cocktails, fundraising dinners—a never-ending succession of opportunities to meet people and forge potentially beneficial links.

To do that had meant working eighteen-hour days, seven days a week. There'd been hardly any down time, and of course it had meant living in London, And that hadn't been compatible with her view of their relationship, or her need to follow her career—although there was no sign of that now.

She'd wanted to stay at university in Norwich,

get her Biological Sciences degree and work in research, maybe do a PhD, but now it seemed she was a virtual PA with a 'very understanding' boss.

So much for her career plans, he thought bitterly.

Hell, she could have been his PA. She would have been amazing, and with him, by his side every minute of the day and night, and Josh would have been his child. That would have been a relationship worth having. Instead she'd chosen her career over him, and then gone on to live her dream with some other man who hadn't had the sense to keep his life insurance going to protect his family.

Great stuff. Good choice, Georgia.

Shaking his head in disgust, he turned away from the door and went downstairs to the kitchen. It was in uproar, the worktops covered with the wreckage of their meal and its preparation, but that was fine. He needed something to do, and it certainly needed doing, so he rolled up his sleeves and got stuck in.

The bath was wasted on her.

It should have been relaxing and wonderful, but

instead she lay in the warm, scented water, utterly unable to relax, unable to shift the weight of guilt that was crushing her.

She got out, dried herself on what had to be the softest towel in the world and pulled on clean clothes. Not her night clothes—she wasn't that crazy—but jeans and a jumper and nice thick slipper socks, and picking up the baby monitor she padded softly downstairs to find him.

The kitchen door was ajar and she could hear him moving around in there—clearing up, probably, she thought with another stab of guilt. She shouldn't have stalked off like that, not without offering to help first, but he'd been so pushy, so— angry?

About David?

She opened the door and walked in, and he turned and met her eyes expressionlessly. 'I thought you'd gone to bed?'

She shook her head.

'I wasn't fair to you just now. I know you cared,' she said quietly, her voice suddenly choked.

He went very still, then turned away and picked

up a cloth, wiping down the worktops even though they looked immaculate. 'So why say I didn't?'

'Because that was what it *felt* like. All you seemed to worry about was *your* career, *your* life, *your* plans for the future. There was never any time for *us*, just you, you, you. You and your brand new shiny friends and your meteoric rise to the top. You knew I wanted to finish my degree, but you just didn't seem to think that was important.'

He turned back, cloth in hand. 'Well, it doesn't seem important to you any longer, does it? You're doing a job you could easily have done in London, that's nothing to do with your degree or your PhD or anything else.'

'That's not by choice, though, and actually it's not true, I am still using my degree. I'm working for my old boss in Cambridge. I'd started my PhD and I was working there in research when I met David.'

'And then you had it all,' he said, his voice curiously bitter. 'Everything you'd always wanted. The career, the marriage, the baby—'

'No.' She stopped him with one word. 'No, I

didn't have it all, Sebastian. I didn't have you. But you'd made it clear that you were going to take over the world, and I just hated everything about that lifestyle and what it had turned you into. You were never there, and when you were, we were hardly ever alone. I was just so unhappy. So lonely and isolated. I hated it.'

'Well, you made that pretty clear,' he said gruffly, and turned back to the pristine worktops, scrubbing them ferociously.

'It wasn't you, though. You weren't like that. You'd changed, turned into someone I'd never met, someone I didn't like. The people you mixed with, the parties you went to—'

'Networking, Georgia. Building bridges, making contacts. That's how it works.'

'But the people were *horrible*. They were so unfriendly to me. They made me feel really unwelcome, and I was like a fish out of water. And *so* much of the time you weren't even there. You were travelling all over the world, wheeling and dealing and counting your money—'

'It wasn't about money! It's never been about money.'

'Well what, then? Because it strikes me you aren't doing badly for someone who says it's not about money.'

She swept an arm around the room, pointing out the no-expense-spared, hand-built kitchen in the house that had cost him ridiculous amounts of money to restore on a foolish whim, and he sighed. 'That's just coincidence. I'm good at it. I can see how to turn companies around, how to make things work.'

'You couldn't make our relationship work.'

Her words fell like stones into the black pool of his emotions, and he felt the ripples reaching out into the depths of his lonely, aching soul, lapping against the wounds that just wouldn't heal.

'No. Apparently not.' He threw the cloth into the sink and braced his hands on the edge of the worktop, his head lowered. 'But then nor could you. It wasn't just me. It needs give and take.'

'And all you did was take.'

He turned then and met her eyes, and she saw

raw pain and something that could have been regret in his face. 'I would have given you the world—'

'I didn't want the world! I wanted you, and you were never there. You were too busy looking over the horizon to even see what was right under your nose.'

'So you left me. Did it make you happy?'

She closed her eyes. 'No! Of course it didn't, not then, but gradually it stopped hurting quite so much, and then I moved to Cambridge and met David. I was looking for somewhere to live and I went into his office, and we got talking and he asked me out for a drink. He was kind and funny, and he thought that what I was doing was worthwhile, and we got on well, and it just grew from there. And he really *cared* about me, Sebastian. He made me feel that I mattered, that my opinion was valid.'

'That was all it took? Kind and funny?'

She gave him a steely glare. 'It was more than I got from you by the end.'

A muscle in his jaw flickered, but otherwise his

face didn't move and he ignored her comment and moved on. 'So what happened to your PhD?'

'I found out I was pregnant, but he'd been moved to the Huntingdon office by then and I was commuting, which wasn't really satisfactory, and then the housing market collapsed. So I contacted my professor and he offered me this job, which kept us going, and then just after I had Josh, David died.'

'And do you miss him?' he asked. His voice was casual, but there was something strange going on in his eyes. Something curiously intense and disturbing. Jealousy? Of a dead man? 'Yes, of course I miss him,' she said softly. 'It's lonely in the house by myself, but life goes on, and I've got Josh, and I'm OK. He was a nice man, and I did love him, and he deserved more from me than I was ever able to give him, but I never felt the way I did with you, as if I couldn't breathe if he wasn't there. As if there was no colour, no music, no poetry. No sense to my life.'

His eyes burned into hers. 'And yet you walked away from me. From us.'

'Because it was *killing* me, Sebastian. *You* were

killing me, the person you'd become. You never had any time for me, we never went anywhere or did anything that didn't serve another purpose. It was all about business, about making contacts that would make more money. I felt like an ornament, or a mistress, someone who should just be grateful for the crumbs that fell from your table. But I didn't want crumbs, I wanted you, I wanted what we'd had, but you shut me out, and you broke my heart, and I never want to let anyone that close to me ever again.

'So, no, I didn't feel for David the way I did for you. I didn't *want* to. He didn't give me what I'd thought I wanted when I was little more than a kid and everything was starry-eyed and rose-tinted, but he loved me, and he took care of me, and he made me happy.'

'And he cancelled the life insurance.'

Damn him! 'He had no choice! We were really struggling—'

'Did he tell you he was doing it? Did you discuss it? Or did he just do it and hope for the best? Because I would *never* have done that to you, Georgia,' he said passionately. 'I would never have left you so unprovided for. Would never have compromised your safety or security like that.'

'You have no idea what you would have done in those circumstances—'

'I know I'd starve before I did that—'

'You have no right to criticise him!'

'You were mine!' he said harshly. 'And you gave him all the things you'd promised me. Marriage. A child. Hearth and home and all of that—hell, George, we had so many dreams! How could you walk away? I loved you. You knew I loved you—'

His voice cracked on the last word, and her eyes flooded with tears; she closed them, unable to look at him any longer, unable to watch his face as he bared his soul to her. Because she *had* left him, and he *had* loved her, but she hadn't been mature enough or brave enough to cope with what he'd asked of her.

'I'm sorry,' she said, her heart aching with so many hurts and wrongs and losses she'd lost count. 'If it helps, I loved you, too, and it broke my heart to leave you.'

She heard him swear softly, then heard the sound

of his footsteps as he walked up to her, his voice a soft sigh.

'Ahh, George, don't cry. No more tears. I'm sorry.'

She felt his hands on her shoulders, felt him ease her close against his chest, and with a ragged sigh she rested her cheek against his shirt and listened to the steady thudding of his heart. His arms closed around her, cradling her against his warmth and solidity, the mingled scent of his skin and the cologne he'd always used wrapping her in delicious, heart-wrenching familiarity.

She slid her arms around his waist, flattening her palms against the broad columns of muscle that bracketed his spine, and he held her without speaking, while their breathing steadied and their hearts slowed, until the tension left them.

But then another tension crept in, coiling tighter, pushing out everything else until it was the only thought, the only reason for breathing.

The only reason for being.

She felt his head shift, felt the warmth of his lips press tentatively against her forehead, and she tilted her head and met his blazing eyes.

CHAPTER FOUR

THE KISS WAS inevitable.

Slow, tender, fleeting, their lips brushing lightly, then gradually settling. Clinging. Melding into one, until she didn't know where she ended and he began.

She curled her fingers into his shirt, felt his fingers tunnel into her hair and steady her head as he plundered her mouth, taking, giving, duelling with her until abruptly, long before she was ready, he wrenched his head back and stepped away.

She pressed trembling fingers to her aching, tingling lips. They felt as if his had been ripped away from them, tearing them somehow, leaving them incomplete. Leaving her incomplete.

She looked up, and his eyes were black as night, his chest rising and falling unsteadily. She could hear the air sawing in and out of his lungs, see the muscle jumping in his jaw as he took another step away.

'I think you'd better go to bed,' he said gruffly, and handed her the baby monitor from the table.

She nodded, her heart thrashing, emotions tumbling one over the other as she turned and all but ran back to her room.

What had she been thinking of, to let him kiss her? After all that had happened, all the water under the bridge of their relationship, everything that had happened since—she must have been mad!

She'd finally found peace, after years of striving, of what had felt like settling for second best—which was so unfair on David, *so* unfair, but how could he compete with Sebastian? He couldn't. And, to be fair to him, she'd never asked him to. But still, it had felt like that, and it was only with Josh's birth and the bond that had formed between them after David's death that peace had finally come to her.

And now Sebastian had snatched it away, torn off the thin veneer of serenity and exposed the raw anguish in her heart. Because she still loved him. She'd always loved him, and now she was hurting all over again, her heart flayed raw by the knowledge of what she'd lost and what she'd done to him, but there was no way she could go back to that lifestyle, to the way he lived and the man he'd had to become.

She changed into her pyjamas and crawled into bed, lying there in a soft cloud of goose down and Egyptian cotton while her thoughts tumbled endlessly and went nowhere.

She heard him come upstairs to bed at something after midnight, but the sound didn't wake her because she was still lying awake, listening to the wind howling round the house, battering the windows with its unrelenting assault. There was no way she was getting out of there any time soon. The lane would be full to the top by now, the snow trapped against the crinkle-crankle wall with no escape, piling up endlessly as the wind drove it off the field.

Trapping her and Josh inside with Sebastian.

Oh, why had she let him kiss her?

Or had she kissed him? She wasn't sure, she only knew it had been the most monumental mistake. It had broken down the barriers between them, ripped away her flimsy defences, opened the Pandora's box of their relationship, and try as they might, they'd never get the lid back on it in one piece.

She closed her eyes. She was *so* not looking forward to tomorrow…

He just couldn't sleep.

Well, there might have been a few minutes here and there, but mostly he just lay awake trying not to think about that kiss while he listened to the wind battering the house and blocking them in forever.

There was no way he was getting her out of here today. No way at all. Which was all made a whole sight more difficult by the fact that he'd let his guard down and weakened like that.

He should have kept his mouth shut, not dragged it all out again. And his voice cracking like that! What the hell was that about? He was *over* her…

Liar.

He sighed harshly. OK, so he wasn't over her, not totally, but he hadn't had to tell her that quite so graphically. He *certainly* hadn't needed to kiss her!

And now they were stuck here, forced together, with no prospect of escape for days. He rolled onto his front and folded his arms under his head, banging his forehead gently on them to knock some sense into himself.

Not working. So he lay there, fuming at his stupidity and resigning himself to a fraught and emotionally draining couple of days ahead.

It could have been worse. At least they had Josh there between them. They could hardly fight over his head, and he'd just have to make sure they were only together when he was around.

Although that was a problem in itself, because Josh, with his mother's eyes and engaging personality, was a vivid and living reminder of all he'd lost when she'd walked away. Josh could have been his son. *Should* have been his son. His first known living relative.

His family.

He swallowed hard, the ache in his chest making it hard to breathe.

It was no good. He'd never get to sleep again. He threw off the covers, tugged on his clothes and went downstairs. If nothing else, he could get some work done.

But he couldn't concentrate, and he ended up in the kitchen making yet more coffee at shortly before six in the morning. He put in some toast to blot it up a bit and give his stomach lining a rest, then sat at the table to eat it.

Not a good idea.

Little boys, he discovered, woke early, and he ended up with company.

Georgia, sleep-tousled, puffy-eyed and with a crease on one cheek, stumbled into the kitchen with Josh on her hip and came to an abrupt halt.

'Ah. Sorry.'

Not as sorry as he was. She was wearing pyjamas, but they were soft and stretchy and the child's weight on her hip had pulled the top askew and exposed an inviting expanse of soft, creamy flesh below her collar bone that drew his eyes like a magnet.

She followed the direction of his gaze and tugged it straight, colour flooding her cheeks, and he dragged his eyes away and jerked his head at the kettle.

'It's just boiled if you want tea?'

'Um—please. And do you have any spare milk? Josh usually has some when he wakes up.'

'Sure. I tell you what, why don't I get out of your way while you do whatever you want to do in here? Just help yourself to whatever you need.'

He left the room with almost indecent haste, and Georgie put Josh down on the floor and let her breath ease out of her lungs on a sigh of relief. She'd forgotten just how good he looked, how sexy, with his hair rumpled and his jaw roughened with stubble.

And tired. He'd looked tired, she thought, as if he'd been up all night. Because of the kiss? Or the wind, hammering against the house until she thought the windows were coming in? Between the kiss and the wind, they'd made sure she hadn't slept all night, and she'd only just crashed into oblivion when Josh had woken.

She hadn't realised it was so early until she saw the kitchen clock, because the snow made it lighter, the moon reflecting off it with an eerie, cold light that seemed to seep through the curtains for the sole purpose of reminding her of the mess she was in.

Why had she let him kiss her?

'Biscuit,' Josh said, and she sighed. They had this conversation every day, but he never gave up trying.

'No. You can have a drink of milk and a banana. There must be some bananas.'

She opened the pantry cupboard and found the fruit in a bowl. She pulled off a banana and peeled it and broke it into chunks for him, and left him kneeling up on a chair and eating it while she made some tea and warmed his milk in a little pan. She would have given it a couple of moments in the microwave, but she couldn't find one. She'd have to ask about that.

She sat down with her tea next to Josh, in the

place where Sebastian had been. He'd left half a slice of toast on the plate, with a neat bite out of it, and she couldn't resist it. She should have finished her supper the night before instead of running out on him, and she was starving.

'Me toast,' Josh said, eyeing it hopefully, and she tore him off a chunk and ate the rest.

'More.'

'I'll make you some in a minute. Let's go and get dressed first.'

She took him upstairs, protesting all the way, and heard water running. Sebastian must be showering, she realised, and tried really, really hard not to think about that, about the times she'd joined him in the shower, getting in behind him and sliding her arms around his waist—

'Right. Let's get you dressed.'

'Then toast?'

'Then I have to get ready, and then you can have toast,' she promised, but she dragged out the dressing and teeth cleaning and face washing as long as possible, then sat Josh on the bed with a book while she washed and dressed herself and tidied the room.

The sound of running water from Sebastian's room had stopped, she realised as she tugged the bed straight. There was no sound at all, no drawers shutting or boards creaking. He must have finished in the shower and gone downstairs again. With any luck he was in the study, and if not, he could show her where the toaster was to save her scouring the kitchen for it.

She retrieved Josh from the bathroom where he was driving the nailbrush around on top of the washstand like a car.

'Toast?' she said, and he beamed and ran over to her, taking her outstretched hand. He chattered all the way down the stairs and into the kitchen, and she was suddenly really, really glad that he'd been with her in the car, that she hadn't been stuck here with Sebastian on her own.

Not with all the fizzing emotions in her chest—

She found the bread, but there wasn't a toaster and he wasn't around. She was still standing there with the bread in her hand and contemplating going to find him when Sebastian came back into the room.

She waved the bread at him. 'I can't find the toaster.'

'Ah. There's a mesh gadget for that in the slot on the left of the Aga. Just stick the bread in it and put it under the cover, and then flip it. It only takes a few seconds each side so keep an eye on it.'

He pulled the thing out and handed it to her, then headed into the boot room.

'I'm just going to check the lane,' he said. 'See how bad it is.'

'Really? It's almost dark still.'

Except it wasn't, of course, because of the eerie light from the snow and the fact that she'd dallied around for so long getting ready.

Even though she'd resisted putting make-up on...

The door shut behind him, and she put the bread between the two hinged flaps of mesh, laid it on the hotplate and put the cover down. Delicious smells wafted out in moments, and she flipped it and gave it another moment and then buttered the toast while the kettle boiled again.

It smelt so good she made a pile of it, unable to resist sinking her teeth into a bit while she worked, and all the time she wondered how he was getting on and what he'd found at the end of the drive.

Sheesh.

He stood inside the gates—well inside, as he couldn't actually get near them without a shovel and a few hours of solid graft—and stared in shock at the lane beyond.

He was already up to his knees in snow and it was getting deeper with every step. Beyond the gates, the snow reached to head height at either side of the entrance. It only dipped opposite the gates because the snow had had somewhere to go.

Straight across the entrance, through the bars of the gates and right up the drive.

There was at least a foot everywhere, but it wasn't smooth and level. It was sculpted, like sand in the Sahara, swirls and peaks and troughs in shades of brilliant white and cold bluey-purple in the light of dawn.

Beautiful, fascinating—and deadly. If he hadn't been here they could have been trapped inside the car, buried alive in the snow, slowly and gradually suffocating in the freezing temperatures—

He shut off that line of thought and concentrated on the here and now. It wasn't good.

In a freewheeling part of his brain that he hadn't even consulted he realised Georgie wouldn't even be able to get away if they landed a helicopter in the field opposite, despite the fact that it was virtually bare of snow now, because the snow in the lane was so deep they'd never cross it. Not that he'd really contemplated hiring a helicopter on Christmas Eve to take her and Josh away and bring his family back, but even if he had…

And the snow wasn't going anywhere soon. Although the wind had finally died away, it was cold. Bitterly, desperately cold, the change from the previous few days sudden and shocking, and he shrugged down inside his coat with a humourless laugh.

He hadn't needed a cold shower. He should have just come out here. Naked. That might have done the trick. The shower certainly hadn't.

He gave the lane one last disparaging look and waded back to the house, walking in to the smell of toast and the sound of laughter, and for a moment he felt his heart lift.

Crazy. Stupid. She left you.

But even so, he'd still have her there for another twenty-four hours at least. More, probably, and nobody was going to worry about this tiny little lane given that it was as bad elsewhere in the county as it was here. He'd already known it, he'd seen it on the news, and only wild optimism had sent him down the drive to check...

He swept the snow which had fallen in through the doorway back out into the courtyard, shut the door, stamped the snow off his boots and put them on the rack, hung up his coat and went back into the kitchen.

She'd made a pot of tea and was sitting at the table with Josh and a pile of hot buttered toast, playing peeka-bo behind a slice of toast. Josh, his face smeared with butter and crumbs, was giggling deliciously and Sebastian felt his heart squeeze.

'Smells good,' he said, rubbing his hands together to warm them, and Georgie looked up and searched his face.

'And the answer is?' she asked, the laughter fading in her eyes, and he shook his head.

'We're going nowhere. The lane's full to head height.'

'Head height?' she gasped, and her eyes looked shocked. As if she was imagining being out there with Josh, trapped in the car, seeing what he'd seen in his mind's eye?

'Hey, it's all right, I was here,' he said softly, reading her mind, and she looked up at him again and their eyes locked.

'But what if…?'

'No what ifs. Don't go there, George.' He certainly wasn't going there again. Once was enough. He took a mug out of the cupboard. 'Any more tea in the pot?'

'Mmm. And I made you more toast. I wasn't

sure if you'd want it but I made it anyway because we interrupted your breakfast.'

He dropped into the chair opposite her and reached for a slice. 'That's fine, I could do with more,' he said, and sank his teeth into it, suddenly hungry.

Hungry for all sorts of things.

Her warmth. Her laughter.

Her little boy, so like her, so mischievous and delightful, a part of her. What did that feel like? To have someone to love, someone who was part of you?

He looked quickly away and turned on the television to give himself something to do.

So much for his defences. They were in tatters, strewn around him like an old timber barn after a hurricane, and she and her child had walked straight through them as if they'd never even existed.

Maybe they hadn't. Maybe they'd just never been tested before, but they were being tested now, with bells on.

Jingle bells.

She was watching the screen, looking at the pictures of snow sent in by viewers of the local breakfast news programme. Not just them, then—not by a long way. And tomorrow was Christmas Day.

'There's no chance we'll be out of here by tomorrow, is there?' she said flatly.

Had she read his mind? Probably, as easily as he'd read hers. They'd always been good at it. Except at the end—

'I think it's very unlikely. I'm sorry. Your parents will be disappointed.' She nodded. Josh was playing on the floor now, driving a piece of toast around like a car, and she met Sebastian's eyes, worrying her lip again in that way of hers.

'They will be disappointed,' she said softly, lowering her voice. 'So will yours. Was it just them coming?'

'No. My brothers were coming up from London—well, Surrey. I expect they'll spend it together now. They live pretty close to each other. What about your family? Was it just your parents, or was Jack going to be there?'

'No, just them. Jack's got his own family now.'

She sighed. 'I really wanted this Christmas to be special. Josh was too small to understand his first Christmas, and last year—well, it just didn't happen really, without David. It seemed wrong, and he was still too young to understand it, so we just spent it very quietly with my parents. But this year...'

'This year he's old enough, and you've moved on,' he murmured.

She nodded. 'Yes. Yes, I have, and he is, and it was going to be so lovely—'

She broke off and swallowed her disappointment, and he couldn't leave her like that. Her, or a little boy who'd lost his father. He had no idea how his own first Christmases had been spent. He didn't even know the religion of his real parents, their nationality, their age. Nothing. Just a void. And he couldn't bear the thought that Josh would have a void where Christmas should have been. He'd make sure that didn't happen if it killed him.

He took a deep breath, buried his misgivings and smiled at her.

'Well, we'll just have to make sure it *is* lovely,' he said. 'Heaven knows we've got enough food, and I've got all the decorations and there's a tree outside waiting to come in, if I can find it under the snow. And we can't do anything else. My family aren't going to be able to get here, and you can't get away, so why don't we just go for it? Give Josh a Christmas to remember.'

She stared at him, taking in his words, registering just what it must be costing him to make the offer—although she might have known he would. The old Sebastian, the one she loved, wouldn't have hesitated. The new one—well, she was beginning to realise she didn't know him at all, but he might not be as bad as she'd feared.

'That would be lovely,' she said softly, her eyes welling. 'Thank you. I know you don't—'

He lifted his hand, silencing her. 'Let it go, George. Let's just take it at face value, have a bit of fun and give Josh his Christmas—no strings, no harking on the past, no recriminations. And no repeats of last night. Can we do that?'

Could they? She wasn't sure, but she wanted to try.

She felt the tears welling faster now, and pressed her lips together as she smiled at him. 'Yes. Yes, we can do that. Thank you.'

He returned her smile a little wryly, and got to his feet.

'So—want to help me decorate the house?'

He gave them a guided tour of the ground floor.

Josh loved it. There were so many places to hide, so much to explore. And Georgie—well, she loved it in a different way, a bitter-sweet, this-could-have-been-ours way that made her heart ache.

No what ifs.

His words echoed in her head, and she put the thoughts out of her mind and concentrated on what he'd done to the house.

A lot.

'Oh, wow!' she said, laughing in surprise when they went into the dining room. 'That's a pretty big table.'

'It extends, too,' he said, his mouth twitching, and she felt her eyes widen.

'Really?' She went to the far end and sat down. 'Can you hear me?'

His smile was wry with old memories. 'Just about. Probably not with the extra leaves in.'

Their eyes held for just a beat too long, and she felt a whole whirlpool of emotions swirling in her chest. She got up and came towards him, running her fingers slowly over the gleaming wood, avoiding his eyes while she got herself back under control. 'Did you get the grand piano for the music room?' she asked lightly, and looked up in time to catch a flicker of something strange in his eyes.

He shook his head. 'No. It seemed pointless. I don't play the piano, but I do listen to music in there sometimes. It's my study now. I prefer it to the library, the view's better. Come and see the sitting room—the old one, in the Tudor part. I think it's probably where I'll put the tree.'

'Not in the hall?'

He shrugged. 'What's the point? I'm never in the hall, I just walk through it. And I thought, over Christmas, we might want to sit somewhere warm and cosy and less like a barn than the drawing room. It's huge, if you remember, and a bit unfriendly. It'll be better in the summer.'

She nodded. It *was* huge, but it was stunningly elegant and ornate in a restrained way, and it had a long sash window that slid up inside the wall so you could walk out through it onto the terrace. She'd loved it, but she could see his point.

In winter, the little sitting room—which was still twice the size of her main reception room—would be much more appropriate. Next to the kitchen in the same area of the house, it was beamed and somehow much less formal than its Georgian counterpart, and it had a ginormous inglenook fireplace big enough to stand inside.

He pushed open the door, and she went in and sighed longingly.

'Oh, this looks really cosy.' Huge, squashy sofas bracketed the inglenook, and there were logs in the old iron dog grate waiting to be lit. She could just imagine curling up there in the corner of a sofa with a book, with a dog leaning on her knees and Josh driving his toy cars around on the floor.

Dreaming again.

'Where are you going to put the tree?'

'In this corner. There's a power socket for the lights, and it's out of the way.'

'How big is it?'

He shrugged. 'I don't know. Eight foot?'

Her eyes widened. 'Will it fit under the beams?'

He grinned and shrugged again. 'Probably. I can always trim it. Only one way to find out.'

'Finding out' turned out to be a bit of a mission. It was in the courtyard, close to the coach house, but the snow was deep except by the back door where it had all fallen in earlier.

'A shovel would make this a lot easier,' he said, standing at the door in his boots and eyeing the snow with disgust.

'I thought you had a shovel in the car?'

'I do. Look at the coach-house.'

'Ah.' Snow was banked up in front of the doors, and digging it out without a shovel wasn't really practical.

'I should have thought of that last night,' he said, but of course he hadn't, and nor had she, because they'd had quite enough to think about already.

She didn't want to think about last night.

She picked Josh up and stood in the kitchen watching through the window as Sebastian ploughed his way through the snow to a huge, shapeless lump in the corner by the coach-house door. He plunged his arm into the snow, grabbed something and shook, and a conical shape gradually appeared.

'Mummy, what 'Bastian doing?'

'He's finding the Christmas tree. It's buried under the snow—look, there it is!'

'Oh..!' He watched, spellbound, as the tree emerged from its snowy shroud and Sebastian hauled it out of the corner and hoisted it into the air.

She went to the boot room door.

'Can I help you get it in?'

'I doubt it. I should stand back, this is going to be wet and messy.'

She moved out of the way, and he dragged it

through the doorway, shedding snow and needles and other debris all over the place. Then he emerged from underneath it, propped it in the corner and grinned at them both.

'Well, that's the easy bit done,' he said. There was a leaf in his hair, in amongst the sprinkles of snow, and she had to stuff her hand in her pocket to stop from reaching out and picking it off.

'What's the hard bit?' she said, trying to concentrate.

'Getting it to stay upright in the stand, and finding the right side.'

She chuckled, still eyeing the leaf. 'I can remember one year my mother cut so much off the tree trying to even it up she threw it out onto the compost heap and bought an artificial one.'

He laughed and turned his back on the tree and met her eyes with a smile. 'Well, that won't happen here. There's no way I can find the secateurs, and the compost heap's far too far away.'

'Well, let's hope it's a good tree, then,' she said drily. 'How about coffee while it drip-dries? And then, talking of my mother, I really should phone her and tell her what's happening.'

'Do that now, although I expect she's worked it out. The news is full of it. The entire country's ground to a halt, so at least we're not alone. And at least you're both safe. There are plenty of people who've been stuck on the motorways overnight.'

'Really?'

'Oh, yeah. It's bad. Go on, ring her, and I'll make the coffee,' he offered, so she picked up the phone and dialled the number, and the moment she said, 'Hi, Mum,' Josh was clamouring for the phone.

'Want G'annie! Me phone!'

'Oh, Mum, just have a quick word with him, can you, and then I'll fill you in.'

'Are you stuck there? We thought you must be. It's dreadful here.'

'Oh, yes. Well and truly—OK, Josh, you can talk to Grannie now.'

She handed over the phone to the pleading child, and he beamed and started chatting. And because he was two, he just said the things that mattered to him.

'G'annie, 'Bastian got a big tree!'

Oh, no! Why hadn't she thought of that? She held out her hand for the phone. 'OK, darling, let Mummy have the phone now. You've said hello to Grannie.'

But he was having none of it, and ran off. 'We got snow, and we stuck,' he went on, oblivious. 'And we having a 'venture, and 'Bastian got biscuits—'

Biscuits. That was the way forward.

She grabbed the packet off the table and waved them at him. 'Come and sit down and give me the phone and you can have biscuits,' she said, and wrestled the receiver off him.

'Hi. Sorry about that. He's a bit excited. Anyway, Mum, I'm really just ringing to say we're stuck here for the foreseeable. The lane is head high, apparently, and there's just no way out, so we aren't going to be able to get to you until it's cleared, and I very much doubt it'll be today—'

'Did he say Sebastian?'

Oh, rats. Trust her to cut to the chase. 'Uh— yeah. He did.'

'As in Sebastian Corder? At Easton Court? Is that where you are?'

'Uh—yeah.' Her brain dried up, and she ground to a halt, but it didn't matter because her mother had plenty to say and no hesitation in saying it.

'I can't believe you didn't tell me last night! Are you all right? Of all the places to be stuck—is he OK with you? And you said "they"—is there someone else there? His family? A woman? Not a woman—oh, darling, do be careful—'

'Mum, it's fine—'

'How can it be fine? Georgia, he broke your heart!'

'I think it was pretty mutual,' she said softly. 'Look, Mum, I know it's not what you want to hear, but we're OK, and we're alive, which is the main thing, and he's being really generous and it's fine. And there's nobody else here, just us. His family were coming today. Don't stress. Nothing's going to happen.'

Nothing more than the kiss they'd already exchanged, but they'd promised each other no repeats…

'You can't just tell me not to stress, I'm your mother. That's what we do! And he's—' Her mother broke off and floundered for a moment, lost for a definition.

'What?' Georgie prompted softly. 'An old friend? And at least we know he's not a serial killer.'

'He doesn't need to be. There's more than one way to hurt someone.'

And didn't she know that. 'Mum, it's fine. I'm a big girl now. I can manage. Look, I have to go, he's made coffee for us and then we're going to decorate the tree. I'll give you a ring as soon as I know what's happening with the snow, OK? And give Dad a hug from us and tell him we'll see him soon. I'll ring you tomorrow.'

She hung up before her mother could say any more, and turned to find Sebastian watching her thoughtfully across the table.

'I take it she's not impressed.'

She rolled her eyes. 'You'd think you were holding us hostage, the fuss she's making.'

'She's your mother. She's bound to stress.'

'That's exactly what she said.' She sat down at

the table with a plonk and gave a frustrated little laugh. 'I'm so sorry.'

'About your mother, who you have no control over, or the weather, for which ditto?' He smiled wryly and pushed the biscuits towards her.

'Here, have one of these before your son finishes them all, and let's go and tackle this tree.'

CHAPTER FIVE

Easier said than done.

It took the best part of an hour to wrestle the tree into the room and get it in the right position, and by the end of it he was hot, cross and had a nice bruise on his finger from pinching it in the clamp.

'Look on the bright side,' Georgie said, standing back to study it critically. 'At least it's a nice soft fir and not a prickly old spruce. And it fitted under the beam.'

He stuck his head out from underneath it and gave her a look. 'Just don't tell me to turn it round again,' he growled, and she smiled sweetly and widened her eyes.

'As if. It looks good. It's even vertical. That's a miracle in itself. So, where are the decorations?'

He worked his way out from under the tree and stood up, brushing bits of vegetation off his cashmere sweater. Probably not the best choice of garment for the task in hand, but with Georgia in the house he didn't seem to be able to think clearly. 'In my study. Come and have a look.'

She followed him to the room that they'd christened the music room, under her bedroom. There was a desk in there positioned to take advantage of the views over the garden, and apart from the laptop on the desk, there was nothing to give away that it was an office. She wondered how much work he did here, or was planning to, or if it was just a weekend cottage.

Some cottage, she thought drily.

There was a stack of boxes beside the desk, and he pulled one of the boxes off the pile and opened it on the desk. 'I'm not convinced they're child-friendly.'

Probably not, she thought, eyeing the expensive packaging. The decorations were all immaculately boxed, individually wrapped in tissue paper and made of glass. Beautiful though they were, she wasn't in a hurry to put them in reach of Josh.

'Not good?' he asked, and she shrugged.

'They're lovely. Beautiful, but they aren't really safe within his reach. He's a bit small to understand about cutting his fingers off.'

Sebastian winced. 'We could put them higher up, out of his reach.'

'We could. And we could decorate the lower part with other things. And they aren't all glass. Look, these ones are traditional pâpier maché, it says. They'll be all right, and I can make gingerbread stars and trees, and decorate them with icing— have you got icing sugar and colourings?'

He raised his hands palm-up and pulled a face. 'How would I know?'

'You put the stuff away in your kitchen?'

He shook his head. 'My mother put a lot of the food away. She was here when it arrived. I was still in London.'

'Ah. Well, in that case we'll have to go and look or be imaginative. There are fir trees in the grounds. We can find fir cones and berries and things—'

'May I remind you that everything in the garden is submerged under a foot of snow?' he said drily, and she smiled.

'I'm sure you'll manage. Coloured paper? Glue? Sticky tape?'

He had a horrible feeling the tree was going to end up looking like a refugee from a craft programme on the television, but then Josh crawled through the kneehole of the desk pushing his stapler along the floor and making 'vroom vroom' noises, and he suddenly didn't care what the tree looked like. He just wanted Josh to be safe, and happy, and together they could have fun making stuff for the tree.

Well, Josh could. He wasn't sure he'd be so thrilled by it, but hey. Josh was just a kid, and Sebastian wasn't going to put his own feelings before the child's. No way.

'Let's put this lot on the top half,' he suggested, 'and I'll go and see what I can find in the garden while you make the biscuits. I'm sure I've got ribbon and sticky tape and coloured wrapping paper left from the presents.'

She smiled, her whole face softening. 'Thanks.

That would be great. OK, Josh, let's go and make the tree pretty, shall we?'

'Lights first,' Sebastian said, picking up the box. 'Do they flash?'

'No they don't,' he said, appalled. 'Nor are they blue. Christmas tree lights should be white, like stars.'

'Stars twinkle,' she pointed out, and started singing 'Twinkle, twinkle, little star', but he'd had enough. Laughing in exasperation, he turned her shoulders, gave her a little push towards the door and followed her back to the sitting room, trying really, really hard not to breathe in the scent of her perfume.

'Your mother rang.'

He paused in the act of tugging off his boots and met her eyes. 'Ah. I sent her a text earlier saying the lane was impassable and Christmas wasn't going to happen tomorrow. What did you say to her?'

She rolled her eyes at him. 'Nothing. I'm not that stupid. She rang the house first, and I heard the answerphone cut in, and then she rang your mobile. It came up on the screen.'

'Right. OK. I'll go and call her.'

'So did you find fir cones and berries?'

'Fir cones. Not berries. The birds were all over them, and I thought their need was greater, but I've got some greenery. I've left it all out here to drip for a bit. Something smells good.'

·'That's the biscuits.'

'Mmm. They probably need testing. Did you make spares?' he asked hopefully.

She shook her head, then relented and smiled at him when he pulled a disappointed face. 'I'm sure there'll be breakages.'

He felt his mouth twitch. 'I'm sure it can be arranged even if there aren't. Stick the kettle on, I'm starving and I could do with a drink. I'll go and call my mother and then we can have lunch.'

He went into the study and picked up the phone, listened to the message and rang her. 'So how is it? Are you cut off, too?'

'Yes, and your brothers aren't here, either. They were coming up last night but of course they watched the news and thought better of it. They're spending Christmas together, though, so they'll be fine.'

'So you'll be alone?'

'Well, we hope not. We were still hoping you might be able to get out with your Range Rover to collect us.'

'No chance. It's head high in the lane and I don't see it thawing with the weather so cold and clear. We're going to have to postpone Christmas for days, I'm afraid. It could be ages before they get through here with a snow plough.'

'Oh, darling, I'm so sorry, how disappointing. And I can't bear to think of you spending your first Christmas there on your own.'

Except, of course, he wouldn't be, but there was no way he was telling her that. 'I'm more worried for you,' he said, hastily moving the subject on. 'I don't know what you're going to eat, I've got all the food here at this end.'

'Well, don't try and keep it. Just have it and enjoy it and we'll worry about restocking later. At least it's only us, and I'm sure I've got things in the freezer. We'll be fine, but be careful with all that food at yours and freeze anything you can't use in time. You don't want to get food poisoning eating it past its use-by date—'

'Mum,' he said warningly, and she sighed.

'Sorry, but you can't stop me worrying about you. Big as you are, you're still my son.'

If only that was true, he thought with a pang, but he didn't go there because he knew that in every way that mattered, he was. Well, his heart knew that, and now, after all these years, he was finally able to accept it. His head, though—that still wanted answers—

He heard a noise and realised that Josh had followed him into the study and was crawling around on the floor with the stapler vrooming again, and he swivelled the chair round and watched him out of the corner of his eye while he listened to his mother making alternative plans and telling him how they were going to get together with the neighbours and it would all be fine, and they'd see him soon.

And then Josh stood up under the desk and banged his head, and started to cry.

'Hang on.' He dropped the phone and scooped Josh up into his arms, cross with himself for not anticipating it so that now Josh was hurt, and cross with Georgia for letting him out of her sight so that it could happen in the first place.

And he was hurt. Real tears were welling in his eyes, and without thinking Sebastian sat back in his chair, cuddled him close and kissed his head better, murmuring reassurance. Josh snuggled into him, sniffing a little, and from the phone on the desk he could hear his mother's tinny voice saying, 'Sebastian? Sebastian, whose child is that?'

Why hadn't he just hung up? But he hadn't, and there was no way round this. He picked up the receiver with a sigh and prepared himself for an earbashing.

'It's Georgia Becket's little boy—'

'Georgie's? I didn't know you were seeing her! How long's this been going on?'

'It's not. It isn't,' he told her hastily. 'She was on her way home for Christmas yesterday afternoon and the other road was blocked so she tried the short cut and got stuck outside the gates. And it was almost dark, so the obvious thing to do was let them stay. I was going to take her home today, but the weather rather messed that up so we're just making the best of it, really.'

Shut up! Too much information. Stop talking!

But then of course his mother started again.

'Oh, Sebastian! Well, thank goodness you were there! Who knows what would have happened if you hadn't been—it doesn't bear thinking about, her and her little boy—'

'Well, I was here, so it's fine, and it's only till the snow clears so don't get excited.'

'I'm not excited. I'm just concerned for her. How is she? That poor girl's been through so much—'

'She's fine,' he said shortly, and then added, 'She's making gingerbread decorations for the tree at the moment.'

Why? Why had he told her that? It sounded so cosy and domesticated and just plain happy families, and his mother latched onto it like a terrier.

'Oh, how lovely! She always was a clever girl.

She was so good for you—I never did understand why you let her go, but you were behaving so oddly then, I expect you just drove her away. I don't suppose you ever talked to her, explained anything?'

He said nothing. He didn't need to. His mother was on a roll.

'No, of course you didn't. You weren't talking to anyone at that time, least of all us.' She sighed. 'I wish we'd told you sooner. We should have done.'

'You should.'

His voice was harsh, and he heard her suck in her breath. 'Well, whatever, you be nice to her. Don't you dare hurt her again, Sebastian, she doesn't deserve it. And—try talking to her. Tell her what was going on then, how you were feeling about the adoption and everything. How you still feel. I'm sure she'll understand. She's a lovely girl and it would be wonderful if you got back together. I'd love to see you happy, and that poor little boy of hers...'

He swallowed hard, pressing his lips briefly to Josh's dark, glossy hair. 'Well, you can put all that out of your head. It's over. It was over years ago, and it's just not going to happen. Look, I'll give you a call when I know more, but in the meantime you take care and don't let Dad overdo it shovelling snow. I know what he's like about clearing the drive.'

'I'll pass it on, but I can't guarantee he'll listen. And I'm sorry we aren't going to be with you, but I'm really glad Georgie is. And her little boy. You'll have so much fun together. How old is he?'

'Two. He's two—well, two and a bit.' *The same age I was...*

His mother sucked in a breath. 'Oh, Sebastian! He's going to love it! I remember your first Christmas with us—'

'Mum, I've got to go. I'm expecting a call. I'll ring you tomorrow.'

He ended the call abruptly and put the phone down, and then swivelled the chair to find Georgie standing there watching him thoughtfully.

'What's not going to happen?'

'Us,' he said shortly, and put Josh back on his feet. 'What can I do for you?'

She could think of a million things, none of which he'd want to hear and all of them disastrous for her emotional security. 'Nothing. I was looking for Josh and I heard him crying. What happened?'

'He stood up under the desk. He's fine now, aren't you, little guy?'

Josh nodded, and she held out her hand to him. 'Lunch is ready when you are,' she told Sebastian. 'Come on, Josh. Let's go and have something to eat.' And she left him to follow them in his own time.

Great. His mother must have heard Josh cry and asked who he was, which would have opened a whole can of worms.

She'd have to apologise for that because it was her fault, of course, for letting Josh run off like that, but she'd been busy rescuing the biscuits from the Aga and one minute he was there and the next he was gone.

Interestingly, though, it sounded as if his mother, unlike hers, wanted them back together. Well, as he'd said, it just wasn't going to happen. It was *so* not going to happen! Been there, done that, and had the scars to prove it.

And so did he, and from the sound of his voice he wasn't any more keen than she was. He'd certainly cut his mother off short when she started asking questions about Josh.

She towed him back to the kitchen and shut the door to keep him there so he didn't cause any more havoc, and sat him down at the table. She'd made cheese and caramelised onion chutney sandwiches, a big pile of them, and there were little golden brown trees and stars cooling on a wire rack on the worktop.

There were even a few failures. Sebastian would be pleased. Or he would have been. Now, with his mother sticking her oar in and putting him on the defensive, things might not be so jolly. She sucked in a deep breath when she heard the door open and forced herself to smile.

'You got lucky,' she told him. 'Some of the gingerbread trees were cracked so we can't use them for decorations. And I found some packets of stock cubes which would make perfect tree ornaments if I wrapped them up. Can you spare them for a few days?'

'Probably. You could take some out just in case we need them, but no, that's fine, go for it.' And dropping into a chair, he picked up a sandwich and bit into it. 'Nice bread.'

She raised an eyebrow at him. 'Well, don't look at me, I just raided the kitchen. It was entirely your PA's choice. I suggest you give her a substantial bonus.'

'I already did.'

She laughed and shook her head, then put the kettle on again to make tea and sat down opposite him. 'I'm sorry I let Josh give me the slip. It must have been—awkward with your mother.'

He rolled his eyes. 'You know what she's like.'

'I do. She loves you, though, even though you fight with her all the time. You do know that?'

'Of course I know that.' He frowned and pushed back his chair. 'Look, I've got work to do, so I might just take a pile of sandwiches and disappear into my study. I'll see you later.'

Oh, great, she'd driven him out. It wasn't hard. All she had to do was mention his mother and it was enough to send him running. She felt her shoulders drop as he left the room, and let out a long, slow breath.

They'd agreed to spend Christmas together and ignore the past for Josh's sake, but the past just kept getting in the way, one way or the other, and tainting the atmosphere, as if it was determined to have its say.

She looked out of the window, but the snow was still there, and it was even snowing again lightly, just tiny bits of dust in the air. Was it ever going to thaw so they could escape?

Not nearly soon enough. She cleared the table, gave it a wipe and smiled at her son.

'Are you going to help me ice the decorations for the tree?' she asked, but he was more interested in eating them, so she gave him a pile of little bits to keep him occupied and piped white 'snow' onto the trees and the stars through the snipped-off corner of a sandwich bag, which seemed to work all right until it split and splodged icing on the last one.

She saved it for Sebastian and took it in to him with a cup of tea, knocking on the open door before she went in.

He didn't seem to be working. He was sitting with his feet on the corner of the desk, his fingers linked and lying loosely on his board-flat abdomen, and he glanced at her and frowned.

'Sorry. My mother just got to me.'

'Don't apologise. It was my fault for not keeping a closer eye on Josh. Here. I messed up one of the biscuits. I thought you might like it, and I've brought you a cup of tea.'

'Thanks.'

He dropped his feet to the floor and sighed. 'I wish this damn snow would clear,' he muttered, and she gave a short laugh.

'I don't think there's any chance. I think it's got it in for us. It was snowing again a moment ago.'

'I noticed.' He looked around. 'Where's Josh?'

'Eating broken biscuits.'

'I thought they were mine?'

'You walked out, Sebastian.'

'Well, it makes a change for it to be me.'

She sucked in a breath, took a step back and turned on her heel and walked away. She got all the way to the door before she stopped and turned back.

'I didn't walk out,' she reminded him. 'You drove me out. There's a difference. And if you had the slightest chance, you'd do it again, right now. But don't worry. The moment the snow clears, I'll be out of here, and you'll never have to see me again.'

'Wait.'

His voice stopped her in the doorway, and she heard the creak of his chair as he got up and crossed the room to her.

She could feel him behind her, just inches away, unmoving. After a moment his hands cupped her shoulders, but he still didn't move, didn't say anything, just stood there and held her, as if he didn't quite know what to say or do but wanted to do something.

She turned and looked up into his eyes, and they were troubled. Hers probably were, too. Goodness knows there was enough to trouble them. She let her breath out on a long, quiet sigh, and lifted her hand and touched his cheek, making contact.

Even though he'd shaved that morning she could feel the tantalising rasp of stubble against her palm, and under her fingers his jaw clenched, the muscle twitching.

'I'm sorry,' he murmured. 'I know it wasn't just you. I know I wasn't easy to live with. I'm not. But—we have to do Christmas for Josh, and I really want to do it right, and I know I said we wouldn't talk about it and I just broke the rule. Can we start again?'

She dropped her hand. 'Start what again?'

He was silent for long moments, then his mouth flickered into a smile filled with remorse and tenderness and pain. 'Christmas. Nothing else. I know you don't want more than that.'

Didn't she? Suddenly she wasn't so sure, but then it wasn't what he was offering, so she nodded and stepped back a little and tried to smile.

'OK. No more snide remarks, no more cheap

shots, no more bickering. And maybe a bit more respect for who we are and where we are now?'

He nodded slowly. 'Sounds good to me,' he said gruffly, and he smiled again, that same sad smile that brought a lump to her throat and made her hurt inside.

How long they would have stood there she had no idea, but there was a crash from the kitchen and she fled, her heart in her mouth.

She found Josh on the floor looking stunned, a biscuit in his hand, the wire rack teetering on the edge of the worktop and a chair lying on its side, and guilt flooded her yet again.

'Is he all right?'

'I think so.' She gathered him up, and he clung to her like a little monkey, arms and legs wrapping round her as he burrowed into her shoulder and sobbed. 'I think he's probably just frightened himself.'

And her. And Sebastian, judging by the look on his face.

He reached out a hand and laid it gently on Josh's

back. 'Are you OK, little guy? You're really in the wars today, aren't you?'

'I've told him so many times not to climb on chairs.'

'He's a boy. They climb. I was covered in bruises from falling off or out of things until I was about seventeen. Then I started driving.'

She gave him a dry look. 'Thanks. It's really good to know what's in store.'

He smiled at her over her son's head, and this time it was a real smile. His soft chuckle filled the kitchen, warming her, and she sat down on the righted chair and hugged Josh and examined him for bumps and bruises and odd-shaped limbs.

Just a fright, she concluded, and a little egg on the side of his head, but that could have been from standing up under the desk.

'Tea?' Sebastian offered, and she nodded.

'Tea sounds like a good idea. Thank you.'

'Universal panacea, isn't it? When all else fails, make tea.'

He put the kettle on and went back to his study to bring his mug and the uneaten biscuit, pausing for a moment to take a few deep breaths and slow his heart rate. He'd had no idea what they'd find, and the relief that Josh seemed to be OK was enormous.

Crazily enormous. Hell, the little kid was getting right under his skin—

He strode briskly back to the kitchen, stood his mug on the side of the Aga so it didn't cool any more and made her a fresh mug.

'How is he?'

'He's fine, aren't you, Josh? It's probably time he had a nap. I usually put him down after lunch for a little while. I might go up with him and read for a bit while he sleeps.'

He frowned as he analysed an unfamiliar emotion. *Disappointment? Really? What was the matter with him?*

'Good idea. I'll get on with my work, and then we'll decorate the tree later.'

'Mistletoe?'

He'd cut mistletoe, of all the things! Like that was *really* going to help—

'I know, I know,' he sighed shortly, 'but it is Christmassy, and everything else was out of reach or too tough, and I could cut it with scissors, and I have no idea where the secateurs might be. I made sure it didn't have berries on, either, in case Josh should try and eat them, because they're poisonous. But there is one bit of holly—for the Christmas pudding.'

She tipped her head on one side and eyed him in disbelief, trying not to laugh. 'The Christmas pudding?'

'Absolutely. You have to have a bit of holly on fire in the middle of the Christmas pudding when it's brought to the table. It's the law.'

She suppressed a splutter of laughter. 'Is that the same law that says that lights must be white? My, aren't we traditional?' she teased, but he just folded his arms and quirked a brow.

'Absolutely. Christmas is Christmas. It has to be done properly. Have you got a problem with that?'

She smiled slowly. 'Do you know what? You've got a good heart, Sebastian Corder, for all you're as prickly as a hedgehog. And no, I don't have a problem with that. Not at all.'

He cleared his throat. 'Good. Right. So, what's next?' he asked, avoiding her eyes and fluffing up his prickles.

Still smiling, she handed him the boxes of stock cubes and a few other little things she'd found that could be wrapped, and they sat down at the table, gave Josh a piece of paper and a pencil to do a drawing, and made little parcels for the tree.

She'd snapped off some twigs from a shrub outside the sitting room window, and once the other parcels were done they made them into little bundles to dangle on the tree.

'Finger,' he demanded, and she put her finger on the knot and he tugged the gold ribbon tight, and made a loop to hang it by.

'You're good at this. You might have found your vocation.'

'I have a vocation.'

'What, making money?'

He sighed and put the little bundle of sticks down on the growing pile.

'George—'

She raised her hands. 'It's OK, I'm sorry, cheap shot.'

'Yes, it was. And I don't just spend it all on myself. I employ a lot of people, and I support various charities and organisations—and I really don't need to explain myself to you.'

She searched his eyes. 'Maybe you do,' she said softly. 'Maybe you always did, instead of just rushing off and doing.'

'Yeah, well, there's been a lot of water under the bridge since then, and as you were kind enough to point out to me when I was asking about David, it's actually none of your business. Now, are we going to finish this tree or not?'

He got to his feet, scooping the little parcels up in his big hands and heading out of the door. She grabbed the fir cones, ribbon and scissors and stood up. He was never going to change, never going to compromise. The word wasn't even in his vocabulary.

'Josh, come on, we're going to decorate the tree,' she told her son, and he wriggled down off the chair and followed her into the sitting room.

CHAPTER SIX

'IT LOOKS GOOD.'

She put the baby monitor on the coffee table, sat down at the other end of the sofa and studied the tree with satisfaction.

Not exactly elegant, with its slightly squiffy little parcels and random bunches of twigs and soggy fir cones—well, the top half wasn't so bad, although there were a few odd bits up there just to link it in so it didn't look like a game of Consequences—but it looked like a proper, family Christmas tree.

And that brought a huge lump to her throat.

Josh had had so much fun putting all their home-made bits and pieces on there, and Sebastian hadn't turned a hair when he'd pulled too hard and the whole tree had wobbled. He'd just got a bit of string and tied it to a hook on the beam above so it couldn't fall.

'It does look good,' she said softly. 'It looks lovely. Thank you.'

Sebastian turned his head and frowned slightly at her. 'Why are you thanking me? You've helped me decorate my tree.'

'And we've done it for my son, which has meant not being able to use all your lovely decorations and smothering the bottom of it in all sorts of weird home-made bits and pieces, which I'm perfectly sure wasn't your intention, so—yes, thank *you*.'

The frown deepened for a moment, then cleared as he shook his head and looked back at the tree.

'Actually, I rather like all the home-made things,' he said after a moment, and she had to swallow the lump in her throat.

'Especially the gingerbread trees and stars,' she said, trying to lighten the moment. 'And don't think I haven't noticed that every time you "accidentally" bump into the tree another one breaks so you get to eat it. Between you and Josh there are hardly any left.'

He grinned. 'I don't know what you mean. And

if we're running out, it's your fault. I told you to make plenty.'

She rolled her eyes and rested her head back against the sofa cushions with a lazy groan. 'This is really comfortable,' she mumbled.

'It is. I love this room. I think it's probably my favourite room in the whole house.'

Because they'd never made any plans for it? Maybe, she thought, considering it. Or had they? Hadn't there been some mention of it being a playroom for all the hordes of children? But they hadn't spent any *significant* time in it. Not like the bedroom. Maybe that made the difference.

Or maybe he just liked it.

She rolled her head towards him and changed the subject.

'So, what's the programme for tomorrow? Since you have such strong opinions on how it should be done...'

Another grin flashed across his face. 'Cheeky.' He hitched his leg up, resting his arm on the back of the sofa and propping his head on his hand so he was facing her, thoughtful now.

'I think that probably depends on you and Josh. What are you going to do about presents for him? Are you going to wait until you're with your parents?'

'I don't know. I don't think so. He was really excited about the tree and he knows there will be presents under it because they had them at nursery, so I think there probably should be something for him to find tomorrow, otherwise it might be a bit of an anti-climax.'

'You don't think it will anyway, with just us and a few presents instead of a big family affair? Wouldn't you rather wait?'

'Do you think I should?'

He shrugged. 'I don't know. It's up to you, but it makes me feel a bit awkward because there isn't one from me, and it'll look as if I don't care and I'd hate him to think that, but obviously I haven't got anything to give him. Either of you.'

She stared at him, unbearably touched that he should feel so strongly about it—and so wrongly. She reached out a hand to him, grasping his and squeezing it.

'Oh, Sebastian. You're giving us Christmas! How much more could we possibly ask? You've opened your home to us, let us create absolute havoc in it, we've taken it over completely so you haven't even been able to work, and—well, frankly, without you we might not even be alive for it, so I really don't think you need to worry about some gaudy plastic toy wrapped up and stuck under the tree! In the grand scheme of things, what you've given him—given us—is immeasurable, and whatever else is going on between us, I'll never forget that.'

Sebastian frowned again—he was doing that a lot—and turned away, his jaw working.

'He's just a kid, George,' he said gruffly.

'I know,' she said softly. 'And for some reason that really seems to get to you.'

He shrugged and eased his hand away, as if the contact made him uncomfortable. 'I don't like to think of kids being unhappy at Christmas. Or ever. Any time. And as I've said, I've got nothing else to do and nowhere else to be. So—presents, or not presents?'

She thought about it for a moment. Her parents

had spoiled him on his birthday just four weeks ago, and he'd had so many presents he hadn't really known what to play with first. And there was nothing here in the house, really, that he could play with safely.

And then she had an idea that would solve it all. 'I think—presents? Or some of them, at least. I've got him a wooden train set, and it comes in two boxes. There's the main set, and there are some little people and a bench and trees and things in another box. You could give him that, if you're really worried about him having something from you under the tree.'

'Don't you mind?'

She laughed. 'Why should I mind? He's still getting the toy, and it would give him something constructive to play with while we're stuck here. And I've got a little stocking for him from Father Christmas. That ought to go up tonight because he's bound to get up early.'

'Does he even know who Father Christmas is?'

She smiled ruefully. 'I don't know. We went to see him, but I'm not sure he was that impressed.

He looked a bit worried, to be honest, but it might make him like the old guy a bit better if he brings him chocolate.'

They shared a smiled, and he nodded.

'You could hang it from the beam over the fire.'

'I could. We might need to let the fire go out first, though, so the chocolate buttons don't melt.'

'Ah. Yes, of course. Good plan. Well, if we let it die down now, it should be all right by the end of the evening. It can go at the side, out of the direct heat. And, yes, please, if I can put my name on the other box of train stuff, that would be good. But you must let me pay you for it.'

She just laughed at that, it was so outrageous. 'You have to be kidding! The amount you're spending on us already? I'll have you know I eat a lot on Christmas Day.'

'Good. Have you seen the size of the goose?'

'We have goose?' she said, her jaw dropping open in delight. 'Oh, wow, I love goose! What stuffing?'

'Prune and apple and Armagnac,' he told her,

and she sighed with contentment and slumped back onto the sofa cushions, grinning.

'Oh, joy. Deep, deep joy. Bring it on…'

He laughed and stood up, slapping her leg lightly in passing. 'That's your job. I have no idea how to cook a goose, especially not in an Aga, so I was hoping you'd do it. Shall I get the presents?'

'I'll come. I only want a few. Where did you put them?'

'In my room.'

Ah.

Was her face so transparent? Because he took one look at her and smiled and shook his head.

'You're perfectly safe, George. I'm not going to do anything crazy.'

No. And wishing she wouldn't be quite so perfectly safe was crazy. Utterly crazy. Good job one of them was thinking clearly.

She nodded slowly and stood up. 'OK. We'll just get the train set boxes and the stocking and leave the rest for when I'm with my parents. Then I can just put the whole bag in the car when I leave.'

* * *

He didn't want her to leave.

It dawned on him suddenly, with a dip in his stomach, as they went upstairs to the bedroom, walking up side by side as if they were going to bed.

And he needed to stop thinking about that right there before he embarrassed them both.

He pushed the door open and flicked on the light. 'They're in here,' he said, and let her through the communicating door into his dressing room. It had been cut in half, the half with the window becoming the bathroom, this half now lined out with wardrobes fitted with racks and shelves and hanging space.

He'd dumped the bag of presents inside one of the practically empty cupboards, and he pulled it out and turned to find her looking around, studying the wardrobes minutely.

'Useful. Really useful. What sensible storage. They're great.'

'They are. How anybody managed with that little cupboard in the bedroom I have no idea.'

'Maybe they didn't have as many clothes. Or maybe they just used it to play hide and seek?' she said lightly.

She was bending over the presents as he held them, and he stared down at the top of her head and tried to work out what was going on in there. Why had she said that? Why chuck something so contentious into the mix?

Although it was him that had raised the subject of the cupboard in the first place...

He had to get out of there. Now.

'Right, why don't I leave you to sort out what you want to bring down, and I'll go and get on. I've got a few loose ends to tie up before tomorrow. Just stick them back in the cupboard when you're done.'

And he handed her the bag and left. Swiftly, before he gave in to the temptation to grab her by the shoulders, haul her up straight and kiss her senseless.

'Here. This is the train set stuff. Did you want to wrap yours in different paper?'

She put the boxes down on the kitchen table and he studied them thoughtfully. 'Does it matter if they're the same?'

'Not necessarily.'

He gave a slight smile. 'I'll do whatever, but I have to say my wrapping paper doesn't really compete with little trains being driven by Santas.'

She smiled back. 'Probably not. And he won't think about the fact that they're the same. He'll just want to unwrap them. He knows what presents are now, having just had a birthday.'

'When was his birthday?'

'Three days after yours.'

His eyebrows crunched briefly together again in another little frown, and she wondered what she'd said this time. Was it because she remembered his birthday? Unlikely. She'd always remembered everyone's birthdays. That was what she did. Remembered stuff. It was her forte, just as his was making money.

She gave up trying to work him out.

'So, lunch tomorrow or whenever we're having

it. Are we going for lunchtime, or mid-afternoon, or evening, or what?'

He turned his hands palm up and shrugged. 'Look, this is all for Josh. I don't care what time we eat, so long as we eat. I'm sure we'll manage whenever it is. Just do whatever you think will suit him best.'

'Lunch, probably, if that's OK? What veg do you have? And actually, where is the goose? It's not in the fridge so I hope it's not still frozen.'

'It's in the larder.'

'Larder?' The kitchen had been so derelict she hadn't even realised it'd had a larder. Or maybe he'd created one?

He walked across to what she'd assumed was a broom cupboard or something, and opened the door. A light came on automatically, illuminating the small room, and she saw stone shelves laden with food. So much food.

'Wow. And this was just for you and your family?'

He gave a wry smile. 'I told you my PA had gone mad.'

Not that mad, she thought, studying the shelves. Yes, there was a lot of food, but much of it would keep and it was only the goose and the fresh vegetables that might struggle.

She shivered. 'It's chilly in here. Ideal storage. I didn't even know it existed. Was it here?'

'Yes. It had one slate shelf and I had the others put in, and it's got a vent to the outside and faces north, which keeps it cool.'

'Which is why it feels like a fridge.'

He smiled. 'Indeed. Perfect for the days when fridges didn't exist. So—there you are. Feel free to indulge us with anything you can find.'

'Oh, I will.'

She ran her eye over it all again, mentally planning the menu, then shut the door behind them and sat back down at the table to write a list.

'Do you really want Brussels sprouts?'

'Definitely. Christmas isn't Christmas without sprouts.'

'And burnt holly.'

'And burnt holly,' he said with a grin.

She bit down on the smile and added sprouts to

the list, then looked up as he set a glass of wine down on the table in front of her.

'Here, Cookie. To get you into the festive spirit.'

'Thank you. And talking of Cookie, are you about to cook, by any chance, or was that a hint for me?'

'I've done it. There's a pizza in the oven and some salad, and we could have fruit or icecream to follow. I thought I'd let you off the hook, seeing as you'll be doing quite enough tomorrow.'

'How noble of you.' She sipped her wine and glanced at her list. 'Is the goose stuffed already?'

'So I was told. Ready to go straight in the oven. It says four hours.'

'I thought you didn't know how to cook it?' she asked drily, and he smiled, his eyes dancing with mischief.

'I didn't want to do you out of the pleasure—and this way you get all the glory.'

'What glory?'

'The glory of basking in my adoration,' he murmured, and she wasn't sure but there seemed to be a mildly flirtatious tone in his voice.

She held his eyes for a startled moment, then gave a slightly strained little laugh and looked away. 'Always assuming I don't burn it.'

'You won't. I'll make sure of that. Right, let's label that present with a new tag, and you go and stick them under the tree and I'll dish up.'

But what to write? His pen hovered for a moment over the tag he'd found. Did it matter? The child couldn't read.

'To Josh from Sebastian' would do.

But he put *love* in there, just because it seemed right. Weirdly right.

'OK, that's done, we need to eat or the pizza will be ruined.'

He slid the box across the table to her, pushed back his chair and made himself busy. So busy he didn't have time to think about what he'd written.

Or why.

She put the presents under the tree while he dished up, and then after they'd eaten and cleared away they peeled sprouts and potatoes and parsnips and carrots, until finally he called a halt.

'Enough,' he said firmly, took the knife out of

her hand, replaced it with her wine glass and ushered her through to the sitting room.

The fire was low, the embers glowing, and they sat there with just the faint glow of the fairy lights and the occasional spark from the fire, his arm stretched out along the back of the sofa, his head turned towards her as they talked about the timetable for tomorrow.

If he moved his fingers just a millimetre—

'Tell me about the renovations,' she said then, and shifted, settling further into the corner, and he reached for his glass and pulled his arm back a little, out of temptation, and as he told her about the house and what he'd had done to it, he watched her and wondered just how much he was going to miss her when she left…

Josh woke early.

He always did, but she'd sat up with Sebastian talking about the house and the building work and what his plans were for the gardens until the fire had died away to ash and her eyes were drooping.

He'd hung the little stocking up on the beam, off

to one side so the chocolate didn't melt, and then he'd taken himself off to his study while she'd come up to bed.

She'd heard him come up later, but not much later, and she'd turned on her side then and fallen sound asleep until Josh's cheerful chatter had woken her.

Bless his darling heart, she loved him so much but she could have done with another half hour. She prised open her eyes and he beamed at her and stood up in the travel cot, holding up his arms.

'Happy Christmas, Josh,' she said softly, gathering him up and hugging him tight. He gave her a big, sloppy kiss, and she laughed and kissed him back and tickled him, then she changed his nappy and took him down to the kitchen.

To her amazement the lights were blazing, the kettle was on and there was a wonderful smell of baking.

And it was after seven! How did that happen?

'Biscuit, Mummy,' Josh said, just as Sebastian came back into the kitchen.

He was wearing checked pyjama trousers and

a jumper, his hair was rumpled and he definitely hadn't shaved, but he'd never looked so good, and her heart squeezed.

No! Don't fall in love with him again!

But then Josh ran over to him and he scooped him up and hugged him, tolerated the sloppy kiss with amazing grace and even kissed him back. 'Happy Christmas, Tiger,' he said, ruffling his hair, and Josh growled at him and made him laugh.

He growled back, and Josh giggled and squirmed down and ran back to her. 'Biscuit, Mummy! Bastian want biscuit too.'

'Ah. Sebastian's actually cooking croissants and pain au chocolat,' he confessed, his eyes flicking to hers in apology.

She smiled. 'It's Christmas. And they smell amazing.'

'They are. And they'll be burnt if I don't take them out. Coffee or tea?'

'Both. Tea first. I'll make it. What do you want?'

'Same. Tea, then coffee. I'll put a jug on for later.'

How domesticated, she thought, getting out the

mugs and making the tea while he rescued the pastries and found plates and butter and jam, and she poured the tea and he sat Josh down and pulled up his pyjama sleeves so he didn't get plastered in butter.

We're like an old married couple, she thought, *just getting breakfast together on Christmas morning, and in a minute we'll go through to the sitting room and open Josh's presents and play with him, and the goose will cook and...*

She cut herself off.

This was a one-off. They weren't married. They were never getting married. And she needed to stop dreaming.

The train set was a hit.

They moved a table out of the way, and Sebastian got down on the floor with Josh and helped him set up the track, and she sat with her feet tucked up under her bottom, still in her pyjamas, cradling a cup of coffee and watching them.

Josh had opened his stocking, with the little cars and a packet of chocolate buttons and a satsuma she'd taken from the fruit bowl, and Sebastian had lit the fire and thrown the peel on it and it smelled Christmassy and wonderful.

So wonderful.

Her eyes filled. What had happened to him to make him change so much, to become so driven, so remote, so focused on something she couldn't understand that their love had withered and died?

He wasn't like that now. Or not today, at least. He'd been pretty crabby out in the lane in the snow, but since then he'd made a real effort.

Or maybe it was just because of Josh, to make him happy. That seemed really important to him, but was there more to it than that?

He'd written 'love from Sebastian' on the gift tag.

Just a figure of speech, the thing everyone always writes? Or because he meant it?

She had no idea, she just knew, watching him, listening to the two of them talking, that he'd really taken her little boy to his heart, and she found it unbearably touching.

'Right. Time to put the goose in,' he said, and

she yanked herself out of her thoughts and put the cup down.

'I'll do it.'

'No. It's heavy. I'll put it in. You can do the tricky stuff later.'

He went out, taking their mugs, and came back a few minutes later with a refill and a handful of satsumas.

'Is that an attempt to compensate for the croissants?' she said drily, and he chuckled and lobbed one over to her, dropping down onto the other sofa and turning so he could watch Josh over the back.

'He chatters away, doesn't he?'

'Oh, yes. He didn't talk very early, but boys don't, I don't think. And they stop talking again in their teens, of course, and just start grunting.'

He frowned again, looking thoughtful for a moment. 'I'm sure I didn't grunt. Nor did my brothers, as far as I'm aware.'

'My brother did. He was monosyllabic for years. It made a refreshing change from all the arguments.'

'How is he? We lost touch when—well, then.'

She ignored his hesitation. 'Fine. He's working in Norwich. He's a surveyor. He's stopped grunting now and he's quite civilised. He's married with two children and a dog.'

He looked away. 'Lucky Jack.'

'He is. He's very happy.'

'I'm glad. Give him my regards.'

'I will. How are your brothers?'

'Better now they've grown up. They both work for me. Andy's an accountant, and Matt's a sales director.'

'Don't they mind answering to you?'

He laughed softly. 'It makes for interesting board meetings sometimes,' he confessed, and she laughed too.

'I'm sure. Talking of families, I ought to ring my parents. They'll want to say Happy Christmas to Josh.'

'How about doing it from my computer with the webcam, so they can see you?'

'Can we? That would be brilliant!'

'Well, since they know you're here, you might as well. Do it in my study.'

She looked down at herself, suddenly aware of what she was wearing. 'I might get dressed first. Just so they don't think we're hanging out all day in PJs.'

And then she looked up, and his eyes were on her, filled with a dark emotion she didn't want to try to understand, and she took Josh upstairs, protesting all the way, and washed and dressed him.

She needed a shower, really, and her hair washed, but she didn't like to let Josh run riot and she could hear water running in Sebastian's room, so she told him to stay there and look at a book, shot into the bathroom and showered and came out to find the door open and no sign of him.

'Josh? Josh, where are you?'

She ran out onto the landing, clutching the towel together, and slammed straight into Sebastian's chest. His bare, wet chest. His hands came up and steadied her, and she stared, mesmerised, as a dribble of water ran down through the light scatter of hair across his pecs and disappeared into the towel at his hips.

'If you're looking for Josh, he's in my room.'

His voice, low and gravelly, cut through her thoughts and she sucked in a breath. *What was she doing?*

He let go of her shoulders and stepped back, and she hitched her towel up and blushed. 'He is?'

'Yes. Don't worry. He came to find me. You take your time, we're fine.'

'Are you sure? Because I really need to—' She waved a hand vaguely at her towel, and his eyes tracked over it and he smiled slightly.

'Yes. You do.'

She glanced down, and saw it was gaping. Dear God, could it get any worse?

Blushing furiously and clutching it together, she went back into her room and closed the door, leant back against it and shut her eyes, humiliation washing over her. How could she have gone out there with her towel flapping open and revealing—well, everything, pretty much!

Not that he'd been exactly covered. Had he always looked that good naked?

Yes. Always. He was more solid now, but he'd always looked good. Tall, broad, muscular, without an ounce of spare flesh on him.

And she really, really didn't need to be thinking about that now! She pushed away from the door, dried herself quickly and wrestled her still-damp body into jeans and a jumper.

Her hair needed careful combing and drying, but it wasn't going to get it.

Or was it? There was a knock on the door and it opened a crack.

'There's a hairdryer in the top drawer of the bedside table. I'm taking Josh downstairs. There's no rush. We're going to play with the train set.'

She sat down on the edge of the bed and sighed. Well, it would give her time to dry her hair properly and put on some make-up. And gather herself together a little. Her composure was scattered in all directions, and she was ready to die of humiliation.

Too right she'd take her time. She was in no hurry to face him again!

Her towel had slipped.

Not far enough. Just enough to taunt him, not enough to see anything. He'd gone back into his room, found Josh under the bed giggling and got dressed before Georgie had time to come looking for him again and caused another incident.

And Josh was more than happy to come downstairs and play with his trains. So was Sebastian. Only too happy, because it reminded him of all the reasons why getting involved with Georgie again would be such a mistake.

She'd walked out on him once, but they'd been the only ones who could get hurt in that situation, and he knew he'd been at least partly responsible. OK, maybe largely responsible, but not solely. He wasn't taking all the blame for her lack of sticking power.

But this time, Josh would be involved. And he was so open, so trusting, so vulnerable. Two was a bad time for your world to fall apart. He knew that, in some deep, inaccessible but intrinsic part of him that still ached with loss.

Wounds that deep never really healed. And that was another reason to keep his distance.

So he played with Josh until she came down, and

then he went into the kitchen and started putting the lunch together.

She followed him, Josh in tow. 'You said I could hook up with my parents,' she reminded him, and he nodded, put the timer on for the potatoes and took her to the study, connected her up and left them to it. Five minutes later they were back.

'I thought I was supposed to be cooking?' she said, but he shook his head.

'Don't worry about it. It actually looks pretty straightforward and the instructions are idiot-proof.'

'Are you sure? I thought that was the deal?'

'There's no deal,' he said shortly. 'Go and play with your son. It's Christmas. He needs you, not me. I'll do this.'

In fact there wasn't that much to do, to his regret. He parboiled the potatoes and parsnips, put them in a roasting pan with some of the goose fat and put them in the oven, moving the goose to the bottom oven to continue cooking slowly.

And then there was nothing to do for an hour.

Well, he had two choices. He could spend his

Christmas Day sitting alone in the kitchen, or he could go back into the sitting room with Georgie and Josh and try not to remember what he'd seen under her towel...

The sitting room won, hands down.

CHAPTER SEVEN

GEORGIE SAT BACK and sighed happily.

'Sebastian, for someone who claims not to know how to cook a goose, that was an amazing lunch. Thank you so much.'

His shoulders twitched in that little shrug of his that she was getting so used to. 'Good ingredients. I can't take any credit.'

That was rubbish and they both knew it, but he'd always been modest about his achievements. For such a high achiever, it was a strange trait, and rather endearing. She smiled at him.

'Nevertheless, it was delicious and I'm washing up.'

'No. The dishwasher's washing up. And the sun's out and it's warmer, so let's not waste the day in here. Has Josh got anything he can wear outside?'

'Yes. Wellies and overalls, in the car, and I brought my wellies, too—hey, we could make snow angels!'

He chuckled. 'I think you'll find if we put him down in the snow, he'll vanish without trace, unless we can find a bit where it's not so deep. Right, let's go!'

So they abandoned the devastated kitchen, wrapped themselves up and headed out into the garden. Sebastian hoisted Josh up onto his shoulders and the little boy anchored his chubby fingers into Sebastian's hair, his happy grin almost splitting his face in half.

'Wait, let me take a photo,' she said, and pulled out her phone. They posed dutifully, and she carried on, snapping off several shots of them as he turned and walked through the archway into the sunlit garden.

And it was glorious. He was right, it would have been criminal to miss it. The wind had died away completely and the sun shone with real warmth, sparkling on the snow and blinding them with its brilliance.

She scooped up a handful of snow and let Josh touch it, probing it with his finger. He was wary, but fascinated, and Sebastian lifted him down on the grass in the little orchard where the snow wasn't so deep and lowered him carefully into it, and Josh watched his feet disappear and giggled.

Then Sebastian turned and looked at her, and she knew what was coming.

She saw it in his eyes, saw the way he carefully gathered up a great big handful of snow and showed Josh how to squash it into a snowball.

'No. Sebastian, no! I mean it—!'

It got her right in the middle of the chest.

'Oh, you rat!' she squealed indignantly, and he just picked up her giggling son and laughed, his head tilted back, his mouth open, his face tipped up to the sun as Josh laughed with him, and if she could have bottled it, she would.

Instead she whipped out her phone and took a photo, the instant before he set Josh back in the snow.

Then she filed her phone safely in her pocket,

because this was war and she wasn't taking any prisoners.

Sebastian's eyes were alight with mischief, and she scraped up a handful and hurled it back, missing him by miles. The next one got him, though, but not before his got her, and they ended up chasing each other through the snow, Sebastian carrying Josh in his arms, until he cornered her in one of the recesses of the crinkle-crankle wall and trapped her.

'Got that snowball, Josh?' he asked, advancing on her with a wicked smile that made her heart race for a whole lot of reasons, and he held her still, pinning her against the wall with his body while Josh put snow down her neck and made her shriek.

'Oh, that was so mean! Just you wait, Corder!'

'Oh, I'm so scared.' He grinned cockily, turning away, and she took her chance and pelted him right on the back of his neck.

'Like that, is it?' he said softly, and she felt her heart flip against her ribs.

But he did nothing, because they found a clear

bit of snow where it wasn't too deep, and one by one they fell over backwards and made snow angels.

Josh's angel was a bit crooked, but Sebastian's was brilliant, huge and crisp and clean. How he stood up without damaging it she had no idea, but he did, and she looked down at it next to Josh's little angel and then hers, and felt something huge swelling in her chest.

And then she got a handful of snow shoved down the back of her neck, which would teach her to turn her back on Sebastian, and it jerked her out of her sentimental daze.

'Thought you'd got away with it, didn't you?' he teased, his mischievous grin taunting her, and she chased him through the orchard, dodging round the trees with Josh running after them and giggling hysterically.

Then he stopped, and she cannoned into him just as he turned so that she ended up plastered against him, his arms locking reflexively round her to steady her.

And then he glanced up. She followed his gaze

and saw the mistletoe, but it was too late. Too late to move or object or do anything except stand there transfixed, her heart pounding, while he smiled slowly and cupped her chilly, glowing face in his frozen hands and kissed her.

His lips were warm, their touch gentle, and the years seemed to melt away until she was eighteen again, and he was just twenty, and they were in love.

She'd forgotten.

She, who remembered everything about everything, had forgotten that all those Christmases ago he'd brought her here, to the orchard where that summer they'd made love in the dappled shade under the gnarled old apple trees, and kissed her.

Under this very mistletoe?

Possibly. It seemed very familiar, although the kiss was completely different.

That kiss had been wonderfully romantic and passionate. This one was utterly spontaneous and playful; tender, filled with nostalgia, it rocked her composure as passion never would have done. Passion she could have dismissed. This…

She backed away, her hand over her mouth, and spun round in the snow to look for Josh.

He was busy squashing more snow up, pressing his hands into it and laughing, and she waded over to him and picked him up, holding him against her like a shield.

'Oh, Josh, your hands are freezing! Come on, darling, time to go back inside.' And without waiting to see what Sebastian was doing, she carried Josh back to the relative safety of the house.

As she pulled off their snowy clothes in the boot room, she noticed the little heap of mistletoe on the floor. It was still lying in the corner where he'd left it yesterday, and she'd forgotten all about it. Had he? Or had he taken her to the orchard deliberately, so he could kiss her right there underneath the tree where it had been growing for all these years? Where he'd kissed her all those Christmases ago?

If so, it had been a mistake. No kisses, she'd said, and he'd promised. They both had. And it had lasted a whole twenty-four hours.

Great. Fantastic. What a result…

* * *

Sebastian watched her go, kicking himself for that crazy, unnecessary lapse in common sense.

He hadn't even put up the mistletoe in the house because in the end it had seemed like such a bad idea, and then he'd brought her out here and they'd played in the snow just as they had eleven years ago, right under that great hanging bunch of mistletoe.

And he'd kissed her under it.

In front of Josh.

Of all the stupid, stupid things…

'Oh, you *idiot.*'

Shaking his head in disbelief, he made his way back inside and found she'd hung up their wet coats in front of the Aga to dry. Josh was playing on the floor with one of the cars out of his stocking, and she was pulling up her sleeves and getting stuck into the clearing up.

'I've put the kettle on,' she said. 'I thought we could do with a hot drink.'

'Good idea,' he said, but he noticed that she didn't look at him, and he only noticed that out of the corner of his eye because he was so busy not looking at her.

No repeats.

That had been the deal. He'd give Josh Christmas, and there'd be no recriminations, no harking back to their breakup, and no repeats of that kiss.

So far, it seemed, they were failing on all fronts.

Idiot! he repeated in his head, and pushing up his own sleeves, he tackled what was left.

'I'm sorry.'

The words were weary, and Georgie searched his eyes.

She'd put Josh to bed, waited until he was asleep and then forced herself to come downstairs. She'd hoped he'd be in the study, but he wasn't, he was in the kitchen making sandwiches with the left-over goose and cranberry sauce, and now she was here, too. Having walked in, there was no way of walking out without appearing appallingly rude, and then he'd turned to her and apologised.

And it had really only been a lighthearted, playful little kiss, she told herself, but she knew that she was lying.

'It's OK,' she said, although it wasn't, because it had affected her much more than she was letting on. She gave a little shrug. 'It was nothing really.'

'Well, I'll have to do better next time, then,' he said softly, and her eyes flew back to his.

'There won't be a next time. You promised.'

'I know. It was a joke.'

'Well, it wasn't funny.'

He sighed and rammed his hand through his hair, the smile leaving his eyes. 'We're not doing well, are we?'

'You're not. It was you that raised the walking out issue, you that kissed me. So far I think I've pretty much stuck to my side of the bargain.'

'Apart from running around in a scanty little towel that didn't quite meet.'

She felt hot colour run up her cheeks, and turned away. 'That was an accident. I was worried about Josh. And you didn't have a lot on, either.'

'No.' He sighed again. 'I have to say, as apologies go, this isn't going very well, is it?'

She gave a soft, exasperated laugh and turned back to him, meeting the wry smile in his eyes and relenting.

'Not really. Why don't we just draw a line under it and start again? As you said, it was warmer today. It'll thaw soon. We just have to get through the next day or two. I'm sure we can manage that.'

'I'm sure we can. I thought you might be hungry, so I threw something together.' He cut the sandwiches in quarters as he spoke, stacked them on a plate and put them on a tray. Glasses, side plates, cheese, a slab of fruit cake and the remains of lunchtime's bottle of Rioja followed, and he picked the tray up and walked towards her. 'Open the door?'

She opened it, followed him to the sitting room and sat down. This was so awkward. All of it, everything, was so awkward, pretending that it was all OK and being civilised when all they really wanted to do was yell at each other.

Or make love.

'George, don't.'

'Don't what?'

He sat down on the other sofa, opposite her, and held her eyes with his. 'Don't look like that. I know it's difficult. I'm sorry, I'm an idiot, I've just made it more uncomfortable, but—we were good friends once, Georgie—'

'We were lovers,' she said bluntly, and he smiled sadly.

'We were friends, too. We should be able to talk to each other in a civilised manner. We managed last night.'

'That was before you kissed me again.'

He sighed and rammed his hand through his hair, and she began to feel sorry for it.

'The kiss was nothing,' he said shortly, 'you know that, you said so yourself. And I'm sorry it upset you. It just seemed—right. Natural. The obvious thing to do. We were playing, and then there you were, right under the mistletoe, and—well, I just acted on impulse. It really, really won't happen again. I promise.'

She didn't challenge him on that. He'd promised to love her forever, and he'd driven her away. She knew about his promises. And hers weren't a lot better, because she'd promised to love him, too, and she'd left him.

What a mess. *Please, please thaw so we can get away from him…*

She reached for a sandwich and bit into it, and he sat forward, pouring the wine and sliding a glass towards her.

'You didn't tell me what you thought of this wine at lunch.'

'Is it important?'

He shrugged. 'In a way. I've got shares in the bodega. It's a good vintage. I just wondered if you liked it.'

'Yes, it's lovely.' She sipped, giving it thought. 'It goes well with the goose and the cranberries. It is nice—really nice, although if it's fiendishly expensive it's wasted on me. I could talk a lot of rubbish about it being packed with plump, luscious fruit and dark chocolate with a long, slow finish because I watch the television, but I wouldn't really know what I was talking about. But it is nice. I like it.'

He laughed. 'You don't need to know anything

else. You just need to know what you like and what you don't like, and I like my wines soft. Rounded. Full of plump, luscious fruit,' he said, and there was something in his eyes that made her catch her breath and remember the gaping towel.

She looked hastily away, grabbing another sandwich and making a production of eating it, and he sat back and worked his way down a little pile of them, and for a while there was silence.

'So,' he said, breaking it at last, 'what's the plan for your house? You say you can't sell it at the moment, but what will you do when you have? Buy another? Rent?'

'Move back home.'

'Home? As in, come back and live with your parents?'

'Yes. I'll have childcare on tap, they'll get to see lots of Josh and I can work for my boss as easily here as I can in Huntingdon.'

He nodded, but there was a little crease between his eyebrows, the beginnings of a frown. 'Wouldn't you rather have your independence?'

She put down the shredded crusts of her sandwich and sighed. 'Well, of course, and I've tried that, but it doesn't feel like independence, really, not with Josh. It's just difficult. Every day's an up-hill struggle to get everything done, hence watching the television when I'm too tired to work any more. There's no adult to talk to, I'm alone all day and all night except for the company of a two-year-old, and after he's in bed it's just lonely.'

The frown was back. 'He's very good company though when he is around. He's a great little kid.'

'He is, but his conversation is a wee bit lacking.'

Sebastian chuckled and reached for his wine. 'We don't seem to be doing so well, either.'

'So what do you want to talk about? Politics? The economy? Biogenetics? I can tell you all about that.'

'Is that what you do?'

'A bit. I don't really do anything any more. I just collate stuff for them and check for research trials and see if I can validate them. Some are a bit sketchy. It's an interesting field, genetic engineering, and it's going to be increasingly useful in medicine and agriculture in the future.'

'Tell me.'

So she talked about her work, about what her professor was doing at the moment, what they'd done, and what she'd been studying for her PhD before she'd had to abandon it.

'Would you like to finish it?' he asked, and she rolled her eyes.

'Of course! But I can't. I've got Josh now. I have other priorities.'

'But later?'

She shrugged. 'Later might be too late. Things move on, and what I was researching won't be relevant any longer. Things move so fast in genetics, so that what wasn't possible yesterday will be commonplace tomorrow. Take the use of DNA tests, for example. It's got all sorts of forensic and familial implications that simply couldn't have been imagined not that long ago, and now it's just accepted.'

His heart thumped.

'Familial implications? Things like tracing members of your family?' he suggested, keeping his voice carefully neutral.

'Yes. Yes, absolutely. It can be used to prove that people are or aren't related, it can tell you where in the world you've come from, where your distant ancestors came from—using mitochondrial DNA, which our bodies are absolutely rammed with, most Europeans can be traced back down the female line to one of a handful of women if you go back enough thousands of years. It's incredible.'

But not infallible. Not if you didn't know enough to start with. And not clever enough to give a match to someone who'd never been tested or had their DNA stored on a relevant database. He knew all about that and its frustrations.

Tell her.

'So, tell me about this bodega,' she said, settling back with a slab of fruitcake and a chunk of cheese, and he let the tension ease out of him at the change of subject.

'The bodega?'

'Mmm. I've decided it's a rather nice wine. I might have some more when I've finished eating. I'm not sure it'd go with cake and cheese.'

'I'm not sure cake and cheese go together in the first place.'

'You are joking?' She stared at him, her mouth slightly open. 'You're not joking. Try it.'

She held out the piece of cake with the cheese perched on top, the marks made by her even teeth clear at the edge of the bite, and he leant in and bit off the part her mouth had touched.

He felt something kick in his gut, but then the flavour burst through and he sat back and tried to concentrate on the cake and cheese combo and not the fact that he felt as if he'd indirectly kissed her.

'Wow. That is actually rather nice.'

She rolled her eyes again. 'You are so sceptical. It's like ham and pineapple, and lamb and redcurrant jelly.'

'Chalk and cheese.'

'Now you're just being silly. I thought you liked it?'

'I do.' He cut himself a chunk of both and put them together, mostly so he didn't have to watch her bite off the bit his own teeth had touched.

Hell. How could it be so ridiculously erotic?

'So—the bodega?'

'Um. Yeah.' He groped for his brain and got it into gear again, more or less, and told her all about it—about how he'd been driving along a quiet country road and he'd broken down and a man had stopped to help him.

'He turned out to be the owner of the bodega. He took me back there and contacted the local garage, and while we waited we got talking, and to cut a long story short I ended up bailing them out.'

'That was a good day's business for them.'

He chuckled. 'It wasn't a bad one for me. I stumbled on it by accident, I now own thirty per cent, and they're doing well. They've had three good vintages on the trot, I get a regular supply of wine I can trust, and we're all happy.'

'And if it's a bad year?'

'Then we've got the financial resilience to weather it.'

Or he had, she thought. They'd been lucky to find him.

'Where is it?' she asked. 'Does Rioja have to come from a very specific region?'

'Yes. It's in northern Spain. They grow a variety of grapes—it's a region rather than a grape variety, and they use mostly Tempranillo which gives it that lovely softness.'

He opened another bottle, a different vintage, and as he told her about it, about how they made it, the barrels they used, the effect of the climate, he stopped thinking about her mouth and what it would be like to kiss her again, and began to relax and just enjoy her company.

He didn't normally spend much time like this, and certainly not with anyone as interesting and restful to be with as Georgie. Not nearly enough, he realised. He was too busy, too harassed, too driven by the workload to take time out. And that was a mistake.

Hence why he'd turned off his mobile phone and ignored it for the last twenty-four hours. It was Christmas. He was allowed a day off, and he intended to take advantage of every minute of it. Tomorrow would come soon enough.

He peeled a satsuma from the bowl and threw it to her, and peeled himself another one, then they cracked some nuts and threw the shells in the fire and watched it die down slowly.

It seemed as if neither of them wanted to move, to call it a night, to do anything to disturb the fragile truce, and so they sat there, staring into the fire and talking about safe subjects.

Uncontroversial ones, with no bones of contention, no trigger points, no sore spots, as if by mutual agreement. They talked about his mother's heart attack, her father's retirement plans, his plans for the restoration of the walled garden, and gradually the fire died away to ash and it grew chilly in the room.

'I ought to go up and make sure Josh is all right,' she said, although the baby monitor was there on the table and hadn't done more than blink a couple of times, just enough so they knew it was working.

But he didn't argue, because they were running out of safe topics and it was better to quit while they were winning and before he did something stupid like kiss her.

He got to his feet, gathered up their glasses and put them on the tray with the plates, made sure the fire guard was secure and carried the tray through to the kitchen.

She was getting herself a glass of water, and he put the tray down beside the sink and turned towards her.

'Got everything you need?'

No, she thought. She needed him, but he wasn't good for her, and she certainly hadn't been good for him. Not in the long term. 'Yes, I'm fine,' she said, and then hesitated.

His eyes were unreadable, but the air was thick with tension. It would have been so natural, so easy to lean in and kiss him goodnight.

So dangerous.

So tempting...

She paused in the doorway and looked back, and he was watching her, his face shuttered.

'Thank you for today,' she said quietly. 'It's been really lovely. Really lovely. Josh has had a brilliant time, and so've I.'

'Even the kiss?'

She laughed softly. 'There was never any doubt about your kisses, Sebastian. None at all.'

'Wrong place, wrong time?' he suggested, and she shook her head.

'Wrong time.'

'And the place?'

'You can never go back,' she said simply, and with a sad smile, she closed the door and left him standing there in what should have been their kitchen, gazing after the woman he still loved but knew he'd lost forever.

'Damn,' he said softly.

It was a fine time to discover that he still wanted her, that he still loved her, that he should have done more to stop her leaving. But his head had been in the wrong place then, and hers was now.

You should have told her.

He should. But he hadn't, and now wasn't the time.

It was too late. She'd moved on, and so had he.

Hadn't he?

He poured himself another glass of wine and left the kitchen, retreating into his study and the thing that kept him sane. Work. Always work. The one constant in his life.

He turned his phone on, and it beeped at him furiously as the emails and messages came pouring in. Even on Christmas Day. He was obviously not the only workaholic, he thought drily, and then he opened them.

Greetings. Christmas greetings from family, friends, work colleagues.

And he'd meant to contact all of them, and so far had only rung his immediate family.

He'd do it now. He had nothing better to do, either, and it beat lying in bed next to Georgie's room and listening to the sounds of her getting ready for bed. Although even in his study he could hear her, because she was immediately overhead.

He listened to the sound of water running, the creak of the boards as she crossed the room to the bed. A different creak as she climbed into it and lay down.

He tried to tune it out, but it was impossible, so he put the radio on quietly. Carols from King's College, Cambridge, flooded the room and drowned out the sound of her movements.

Pity they couldn't drown out his thoughts…

CHAPTER EIGHT

'Mummy! Mummy, wake up!'

She prised her eyes open. Light was leaking round the edges of the curtains, and it looked—astonishingly—like sunlight. She propped herself up on one elbow and scraped her hair back out of her eyes.

'Hello, Mummy!'

He was beaming at her, and she felt her heart melt. 'Hello, darling. Are you all right? Did you sleep well?'

He nodded vigorously. He was standing in the cot, bobbing up and down with unchannelled energy, and he looked bright-eyed and bushy-tailed.

'Want Bastian,' he said. 'Play in snow.'

The cot rocked wildly, and she sat up and grabbed the edge to steady it. 'Let's get up first, shall we? Nappy, drink, clothes on? Then we'll see.'

He nodded and held up his arms, and she lifted him out. He was warm and he smelled of sleepy baby, and she breathed him in and snuggled him close for a moment, but he wasn't having any of it. There was snow outside with his name on it, and he wanted out.

Now.

She changed his nappy, hesitated for a moment and pulled on his clothes, then dressed herself quickly, just in case Sebastian was around. That almost-kiss last night was still tormenting her as it had been all night so she wasn't going to tempt fate, but Josh was starving and in a hurry.

Teeth and a quick wash could wait till after breakfast, she decided, and opened the bedroom door to the wonderful smell of bacon cooking. And toast, the aromas wafting up the stairs and making her mouth water.

He turned as she went in, frying pan in hand, and smiled at them. 'You're up bright and early.'

'Well, someone is,' she said drily, as Josh ran

over to Sebastian and put his arms round his legs, tilting his head back and looking up pleadingly.

'Want snow,' he said, and Sebastian gave a slightly stunned laugh.

'Whoa, little fella, it's a bit early for that. How about some nice breakfast first?' He looked across at Georgie. 'Does he like bacon sandwiches?'

She laughed. 'Probably. He's never had one, but he likes bacon and he eats sandwiches. And I certainly do.'

His smile was a little twisted, his voice soft. 'I know.'

Of course he did. They'd had bacon sandwiches for breakfast every Sunday morning when they'd been together, either at home or in a café. And he hadn't forgotten, apparently, any more than she had.

Those dangerous emotions swirled in the air for a moment, carried, like the memories, on the smell of frying bacon, and she pulled herself together with an effort.

'Can I do anything?' she asked briskly. 'Make tea? Coffee?'

'Tea. I've had coffee. I've been up a couple of hours.'

'Really?'

She glanced at the old school-style clock on the wall and did a mild double-take.

'It's after eight! When did that happen?'

'While you were sleeping?' he said, his eyes gently mocking. 'I was about to come up and open the bedroom door when I heard Josh chatting. I knew you wouldn't be long if I let the smell of bacon in.'

'Like one of Pavlov's dogs?'

'If the cap fits...'

'You are so rude.' She stared at the worktop blankly. 'What was I doing?'

'Making tea?' he offered, his mouth twitching, and she threw the tea towel at him and put the kettle on while he moved the bacon to the slower burner and sliced some bread.

In the time it took her to make the tea and give Josh a drink of milk, he'd flipped the bacon out onto kitchen paper to drain, cracked some eggs into a pan and scrambled them while the toast cooked, sliced some tomatoes, split the toast and made a stack of club sandwiches.

'He might be happier with bread,' she said, but Josh reached out, his little hand opening and closing frantically. 'Me have Bastian sandwich,' he said.

He was getting a serious and rather worrying case of hero worship, she realised with a sigh, but she shrugged and cut him off a chunk. She didn't think he'd eat it, but he did, and demanded more.

'I'm not sure I'm going to give him any more, this is soooo good,' she mumbled through a mouthful, and Sebastian just laughed and handed Josh the rest of his own.

Just like a father would.

She blinked, sucked in a quiet breath and gave herself a mental shake. He was *not* Josh's father, and he wasn't going to be his stepfather, or surrogate father, or even a best uncle! He was nobody to Josh except an old friend of hers who'd rescued them one Christmas, and that was the way it had to stay if she didn't want to risk him getting hurt. Hero worship notwithstanding.

Frankly, he'd lost enough already. And so had she.

'Right, I'm going out to clear the drive. The snow's beginning to soften slightly. It didn't freeze last night, and with the sun on it the drive might thaw if I can get most of the snow off it. I wouldn't be surprised if they don't clear the lane tomorrow.'

'Not today?' she asked, sort of hopefully, although a part of her definitely didn't want it cleared yet.

'Not on Boxing Day,' he said. 'It's unlikely. They'll be clearing the main roads still, making sure the urban areas are safe for the majority of the population. This lane is incredibly small potatoes in comparison. It's probably not even on their to-do list so it might be a local farmer.'

She nodded slowly. That made sense, and if the farmer had stock, he might be too busy with them to worry about the lane for days.

And she wasn't at all sure how that made her feel.

Yes, she was!

She had to get out of here before—well, before it got any worse. Before Josh's idolisation of Sebastian got out of proportion. And before one or other of them cracked big-time and gave into the magnetic tug of attraction that time didn't seem to have done anything to weaken. And that meant being able to get the car out.

'If you've got another shovel, can I give you a hand?'

'I haven't, but you can come out and cheerlead if you like. I'm sure Josh'll have fun out there playing in the snow, won't you, Josh? There aren't any roses or anything lurking under the snow to hurt him, not near the drive, so he can't come to any harm.'

'Me snow!' he begged, bouncing up and down beside her, his eyes pleading, and she gave up the unequal struggle. They didn't have to stay out there for long.

'Teeth first, and then we'll go outside. OK?'

'OK!'

He ran off, heading towards the stairs, with

Georgie in hot pursuit, and as they left the kitchen Sebastian found himself smiling.

Why?

Because he was happy?

Because they were coming outside to help him clear the drive, and he'd get to play with Josh again?

Not to mention Georgie...

Stop it!

They could make a snowman, he thought, dragging his mind back to the child, and he tracked down a carrot for his nose and two Brussels sprouts for eyes, then wrapped up warm and went outside to get started.

The snow wasn't quite as deep as it had been, but there was still quite enough of it and the first thing he did was cut a path through to the gates and clear around the bottom of them so they had room to swing open.

Assuming the mechanism wasn't frozen solid. It had better not be, he'd paid enough for them to be restored and the electric openers to be fitted.

He wouldn't test them. Not yet, not until the sun

had time to get on them and warm them up a little, but he could clear the rest of the snow from in front of them.

He'd hardly started when Georgie and Josh arrived. He'd heard them coming, Josh's excited chatter reaching him long before Georgie's mellow tones.

'How are you doing?'

'OK. It's slow.'

'Is it OK if we build a snowman?' she asked.

He straightened up and turned to look at them. Josh was busy making a snowball, crouched down with his little bottom stuck out and perched on the snow, and Georgie, bundled up in her coat and gloves, looked so like she had all those years ago when they'd played in the orchard right here that his heart tugged.

He pulled out the carrot and sprouts. 'Great minds think alike,' he said with a smile, and handed them to her.

'What's that?' Josh asked, peering at them, the snowball forgotten.

'His nose and eyes,' he said, and got a sceptical

look, but Georgie just laughed, the sound rippling through him like a shock wave.

'You'll see, Josh. Now, where shall we build him?'

'Over there?' Sebastian suggested, pointing at a piece of ground he knew was firm and flat, so they went over to it, and she started rolling up a ball to make the body while he carried on shovelling the drive.

'Gosh, it's heavy!'

He turned to watch her. She was shoving it with both hands, and after a moment her feet slipped and she face-planted into the snow.

He had to laugh.

He couldn't help it, and nor could Josh, the laughter bubbling up inside them irresistibly, but then he relented and went over and held out a hand, hauling her to her feet.

Her eyes were laughing, even though she was pretending to be cross with them, and she brushed herself off and straightened, just inches from him. There was a trickle of melting snow on her cheek, and he wiped it gently away with his thumb.

Their eyes met and locked, and for a moment time seemed suspended. Then Josh floundered over to them, and the spell was broken, and he breathed again.

'Need a hand with your snowman?' he asked.

'I never turn down muscle when it's offered,' she said, and he chuckled.

'I take it that's a yes,' he said and, abandoning the shovel, he joined in the fun.

'There!'

He'd rolled up a smaller ball for the head, heaved it on top of the body and set it in a little hollow so it didn't rock off, and she'd pushed in the carrot and sprouts to make his face and found a stick for a pipe.

They were standing back to admire their handiwork, and Georgie frowned.

'He needs a scarf,' she said, and he shrugged and unravelled the scarf from round his neck.

She blinked. 'I can't use that,' she said, sounding scandalised. 'It's a really nice one. It feels like cashmere.'

He shrugged again. 'It's fine.'

It meant he wouldn't have one until the snow went, but that didn't matter. He could rescue it then, and it could be washed. Even if it got ruined, which it probably would, he realised he didn't care.

Didn't care at all, because Josh was giggling and having a brilliant time, and that was all that mattered.

But then the brilliant time came to an end. His fingers were cold, his nose was bright red and he was hungry, and Georgie took him back inside, leaving Sebastian to his shovelling.

He studied the drive, assessing the task.

Monumental, really. He would be there all day, but it needed doing, and the hard physical exertion was a distraction from his thoughts.

It worked well, until he had to stop for a while, straightening up with a groan and shoving his hands in the small of his back and arching it out straight.

'Ouch.' Clearly not as fit as he imagined he was.

He turned to look at the snowman, and found himself smiling.

His eyes weren't on the same level, his nose was bent, his head wasn't quite in the middle, but the scarf looked good.

He gave a wry huff of laughter. So it should, but it had been worth it just to see the little boy's face. And Georgie's.

He felt a wash of emotion that he didn't really want to analyse. It felt curiously like happy families, and it felt good, and that wasn't a great idea. Not at all.

Damn. It's not going to happen. Don't go there.

He went back to the shovelling, working until the burning in his back muscles forced him to stop. He creaked up straight, studied the drive again and shrugged.

The gates had opened when he'd tested them, and the area beyond the gates was cleared, as was the drive for the first thirty or so feet. His car would get through the uncleared bit if he took it steady. All he needed now was for the farmer to come and clear the lane, and he was home free.

Or, rather, she would be.

He ignored the stab of something that he didn't

want to think about, and headed inside into the warm. Not that his body was cold, but his nose and ears were a bit chilly and his hands were cold where the gloves had got soaked making the snowman.

With any luck, he thought as he kicked off his boots, Georgie and Josh would be in the little sitting room and he could go straight into his study and distract himself in there.

They weren't. They were in the kitchen, Josh playing on the floor with a little car, and the air was full of the aroma of freshly brewed coffee.

She walked over to the boot room door and leant on the frame with a smile. 'You've saved me a journey,' she said. 'I was just about to bring you a drink.'

'I'm done. My back aches and I've cleared enough.'

She tsked under her breath. 'I knew you'd do too much. Where does it hurt? Do you want me to rub it for you?'

He gave her an incredulous look. 'I don't think that's a good idea.'

'But you're hurting.'

He sighed softly and met her eyes, his dark with all manner of nameless emotions that made her heart lurch in her chest. 'Let me put it in words of one syllable,' he said slowly. 'I am trying—'

'That's two,' she said, trying to lighten the stifling atmosphere.

He rolled his eyes. 'OK,' he said, his voice ultrasoft so Josh wouldn't hear. 'I. Need. To. Keep. My. Hands. Off. You. And. If. You. Touch. Me. That. Will. Not. Help!'

And without waiting for her to make some sassy reply, he cupped her shoulders in his hands, moved her out of his way and forced himself to walk away from temptation.

Georgie closed her eyes and blew out her breath slowly.

What an idiot she was! Of course he didn't want her touching him! It was hard enough as it was. Throw any more fuel on the fire between them and it would rage out of control like a bushfire. And neither of them needed that.

Yes...!

No! No, no, no, no, NO!

She poured a coffee for him, told Josh she would only be a moment and followed him to his study, her heart pounding.

She knew he was there because the music was on and she could hear it from the kitchen doorway. She tapped, pushed the door open and went in, leaving the door open for safety.

'Coffee,' she said, setting it down on the mat on his desk, and he turned his head and looked up at her.

'George—I'm sorry. It's just...'

'I know. It's my fault. I wasn't thinking. I'll see you later for lunch. Half an hour OK?'

He nodded. 'That would be great. Thanks.'

She took herself back to the kitchen, poured a coffee for herself and took Josh back into the little sitting room to play with the train set for a few minutes. It was nearer to Sebastian, but they weren't making a lot of noise and she didn't think they'd disturb him, especially not over the music.

But then the door opened and he came in, cup in hand, and joined them.

Why?

Because he couldn't stay away?

'I've just spoken to the local farmer. He's going to clear the lane. He'll make a start today, but it might be tomorrow before he gets to the gate.'

'Oh. Right.' She forced a smile. 'Well, that's good to know. I'll tell my mother to expect us.'

'So—shall I get lunch?'

'Goose sandwiches?' she teased, but he shook his head.

'We had sandwiches for breakfast and for supper. It might be time for something more imaginative. We have a whole groaning larder to choose from.'

They did.

She made a winter salad tossed in a honey and mustard dressing to go with the goose which he shredded and crisped in the oven, and Josh had a little of it with some pasta and pesto and a handful of cherry tomatoes.

'That was nice and healthy,' she said, and he laughed and got out the Christmas cake.

'It was. And I'm starving. You can be too healthy. Want cheese with it?'

'Mmm. And tea.'

She cubed some cheese for Josh, gave him a sliver of the cake without icing and then cut them both a chunk.

Sebastian was munching his way through a slab the size of his hand when he glanced up and frowned.

'It's raining!'

'What?'

She turned and looked out of the window.

Rain. Only light rain, but rain, not snow. And that meant a sudden thaw.

'It could flood tomorrow,' she said.

'It could, if it keeps on. In the meantime, I guess my activities on the drive are over.'

'Well, it won't be necessary anyway if it's going to rain hard. It's a pity, though. I was hoping I could take Josh outside again for a bit more running around.'

Sebastian shrugged. 'There's plenty of room in the house. He can run around in here, can't you, Josh?'

'Well, that's true,' she said. 'If he just tears up and down the hall he'll wear himself out in half an hour.'

'Play hide and seek?' Josh said hopefully, and Sebastian smiled indulgently at him.

'Sure. Heaven knows there are plenty of places to hide,' he said drily, his eyes flicking up to Georgie's.

There were. More than enough. And she'd hidden in all of them, and he'd found her.

And kissed her.

She looked hastily away.

'I think we could stick to the ground floor.'

'Or the attic?'

'The attic? Have you done anything with it?'

'Not much. It's been cleaned out and repaired when the roof was sorted, but it's pretty much as it was. I thought the house was big enough for me with just two floors.'

'What's a tick?' Josh asked, looking puzzled, and Georgie suppressed a smile.

'Not a tick, an attic. It's—well, we'll show you, shall we? It's just the very, very, very upstairs.'

'Oh.'

Sebastian chuckled softly. 'I can hear the cogs turning.'

'Oh, yeah. Watching him learn is amazing. Let's go and show him.'

He opened the door at the top of the stairs, and Georgie followed him and looked around, her eyes wide.

'Gosh. It looks enormous now you can see it all. It used to be full of cobwebs and birds' nests and clutter.'

'It was—especially the clutter. We lost count of the number of skips it took to take it all away.'

'Was there anything interesting?'

'There was, but most of the stuff was damaged because the birds had got in. I've got some of the things that were rescued downstairs, but most of it was beyond saving. And there was a lot of rubbish. You know what people are like. They put stuff away and leave it "just in case", and then forget it.'

She walked slowly through the rooms, Josh's hand firmly in hers, and checked that it was safe. It was. There was nothing that could harm him, and so she let go of his hand.

'Right. Are we going to play hide and seek?'

'Yay! Hide and seek! Yay!'

Josh was bouncing on the spot, and she put her hands over her eyes and peeped through her fingers.

'You peeping!' he said, and she laughed.

'I'm going to count. Josh, Sebastian, go and hide!'

He grabbed Josh by the hand and grinned. 'Come on. I know a good place.'

He did. It was under the eaves, behind the chimney, and he pulled Josh in there and held him close.

'Ready or not, here I come!'

He could hear her footsteps coming, and Josh started to giggle.

'Shh,' he whispered. 'Don't make a sound.'

He could hear her footsteps coming, going into another room, then coming closer, closer...

Like the walls, closing in on him, the small boy leaning on his leg, a voice saying 'Shh,' the sound almost inaudible in the silence.

Silence broken only by the sound of footsteps...

A sudden wave of panic came out of nowhere, and he tried to swallow it, but it wouldn't subside, and with a sudden rush he straightened and burst out of the tight space and into the light.

'Sebastian?'

She was right there, staring at him curiously, her mouth moving, but he could hardly hear her through the pounding of his heart. It was running like an express train, deafening him, and he made some vague excuse about having something to do and walked swiftly away on legs like overcooked spaghetti.

Georgia stared after him.

Busy? It was Boxing Day, all businesses except retail outlets were closed.

No. It was just an excuse not to be with her and Josh. Maybe he felt she was just sucking him in again?

But it had seemed like more than that. Much more. There had been something in his eyes...

No matter. He'd left, claiming pressure of work, and so she left him to it and played with Josh for a while, hiding in easy to find places, making enough noise to give him a clue, and they giggled and hugged and had fun.

And all the time, in the back of her mind, was Sebastian. And she was troubled, for some reason.

'Right, that's enough of hide and seek. It's very dirty up here. Shall we go and play with your train again?'

'Bastian play with me?'

'No, darling, he's busy, but I will. Of course I will.'

But first, she had to find Sebastian. She sorted Josh out, settled him down with the train set and went to find him.

He was in the study, of course, doing something on his computer, and he glanced up at her and carried on.

'OK, what's going on?'

'Nothing. I'm fine. I'm just busy.'

'No, you aren't. Sebastian, talk to me. What's the matter? What happened back there?'

'Nothing. I just don't like being shut in. You know that. It's why I never go in a lift.'

'I know, but—'

'But nothing. It's fine.'

'It's not fine. You ought to see someone about that,' she told him softly. 'They can do things about claustrophobia.'

'I take the stairs. It's good for me.'

'But—'

'Georgia, leave it.'

Georgia. Not George, not Georgie.

She hesitated a moment, then gave a defeated little shrug and walked away. He was shutting her out again, shutting her out as he always did.

Well, she was tired of fighting him. With any luck the rain which she'd heard gurgling in the gutters was washing away the snow on the roads, and first thing in the morning, as soon as the lane was clear, she was off, because she just couldn't do this any more.

He didn't appear again that day. She cooked supper for Josh, then took him up and bathed him and put him to bed, and when she came down she could see that Sebastian had helped himself to something.

A goose sandwich, ironically, she thought from the evidence left scattered about on the worktop. And carefully timed for when she was out of the way.

She shrugged. Oh, well, if he didn't want her company, she wasn't going to force it on him. And even though she didn't really need another sandwich, she made herself one and ate it at the table. Just in case he was in the little sitting room.

He wasn't.

She realised that after she'd finished her sandwich and cleared up the kitchen. She'd made a cup of tea, and picking up the baby monitor she went out into the hall. It was dimly lit, and she could see light coming under the study door, but the door to the little sitting room was open and it was dark inside.

Fair enough. She'd sit in there, watch the television and start packing up Josh's toys.

Once the lane was cleared, she didn't want to be here a minute longer than necessary. They'd clearly outstayed their welcome, and she felt emotionally exhausted.

So exhausted, in fact, that she went up to bed as soon as she'd dismantled the little train set. Josh didn't stir when she went in, and she turned off the monitor, put it down on the bedside table and got ready for bed in the bathroom.

She would have liked to read, but her book was in the car and anyway she doubted she'd be able to concentrate. She lay down, closed her eyes and tried not to think about him, but it was impossible.

Her mind was full of images—him playing in the snow with Josh, shovelling snow, laughing at her as she fell on her face, kissing her under the mistletoe—and coming out from behind the chimney in the attic as if the hounds of hell were after him. He'd always been claustrophobic, but it had looked like more than that.

No. He'd never liked being shut in. He never went in lifts, as he'd reminded her, and he'd never hidden anywhere cramped when they'd been playing hide and seek.

He'd been rubbish at hiding. Good at finding, but rubbish at hiding. And he'd been hiding with Josh, in behind the chimney. It was tight in there, tight and dark, and although she'd never been afraid of it, she could see why he might have been.

Well, it had been his idea to go in the attic, and a bit of claustrophobia wasn't going to have kept him holed up in his study for the rest of the day.

No, he was sick of them being there, interrupting his routine, cluttering up his house and his life and just generally taking over. Well, just a few more hours and she'd be gone. She'd looked out of the bathroom window and the snow was patchy already. By the morning, it would be clear and she could get away.

And she wouldn't need to see him again.

* * *

The noise woke her.

Not a scream, more of a muffled shout, a cry of pain.

Sebastian.

She grabbed the baby monitor and tiptoed out of the room, closing the door behind her. His door was never completely closed, but as she opened it further she could hear him breathing fast, muttering in his sleep, wordless sounds of distress.

The dream again. 'Sebastian?'

She switched on the bedside light and reached for him, shaking his shoulder gently.

'Sebastian? Wake up. It's a dream. It's just a dream.'

His eyes flew open and locked on hers, and then he turned away, throwing his arm up over his eyes, his chest heaving.

He looked awful. His face was ashen, his eyes wary, and he was breathing hard, as if he'd been running, and it shocked her.

'Sebastian?'

She reached out a hand and touched him tentatively, and he dropped his arm and dragged a hand down over his face.

'I'm all right. I didn't mean to disturb you. Go back to bed.'

'You had the dream again, didn't you?'

He swallowed hard.

'I'm fine.'

'No, you're not. Do you want a cup of tea?'

He shook his head. 'No. You need to be with Josh.'

But he was shaking all over, his skin grey, and she turned on the baby monitor and put it on the bedside cabinet, then got into bed beside him and pulled him into her arms.

'It's OK,' she said, murmuring to him as she would to Josh. 'It's OK. I've got you.'

He shuddered, and then slumped his head against her shoulder, letting the tension out of his body in a rush. 'I'm sorry.'

'Don't be. I wish you'd talk to me.'

'No. I don't want to talk about it.'

But he needed her, and she was there, just there, in his bed, in his arms, and he gave up fighting.

His hand came up and cradled her face, his fingers still shaking, and then his mouth was on hers, her body under his, her hands running over him as she made desperate little pleading noises.

He lifted his head and she followed him, her mouth searching for his, her lips clinging, and he followed her back down to the pillow and let go of the last shred of his self-control.

CHAPTER NINE

WHEN HE WOKE in the morning, he was alone.

Had he dreamed it?

Dreamed it all, not just *the dream*—hell, he hadn't had it for ages, but last night—and then afterwards...

Had she come to him?

No.

Or had she? It had seemed so real...

He rolled his face into the pillow and breathed in, and the faint, lingering scent of her perfume dragged him right back to the dream.

No. Not the dream. The thing that wasn't a dream. The thing that had been a really, really bad idea.

Damn.

He rolled onto his back and stared at the ceiling. It was dark outside, and he could hear the rain falling, but his watch had beeped ages ago which meant it was long after six.

He peered at the hands. Six forty-eight. Nearly seven.

He threw back the bedclothes and hit the shower, standing under the pounding blast and letting it wash away the fog of fear and confusion that lingered in the corners of his mind.

And with the washing away of the fog came clarity, and with it, the realisation of just what he'd done.

He must have been crazy! How could he have let himself do that? Of all the stupid, stupid things—

He turned off the water and stepped out, burying his face in the towel for a long moment before towelling himself roughly dry.

He heard something—machinery?—and strode to the window, yanking the curtain out of the way.

There were lights on the lane; a tractor, clearing the snow in the almost-dark. The drive looked almost completely free of snow.

Which meant Georgie could leave.

Good. That was good, he told himself, but it

didn't feel good, and just underlined how big a mistake he'd made last night. Well, never again. He was done with breaking his heart over Georgia Beckett.

He was up.

She could hear him moving around in his room, hear the water running. Josh was playing on the floor, and she'd showered and dressed and she was packing their things.

His cot, with the bedding Sebastian had lent her. All their wash things. Random toys and bits and pieces scattered about all over the room by Josh.

She checked under the bed and found the nappy cream she'd lost last night, and put it in the changing bag. Time he was potty trained, anyway. She'd do that as soon as she was home, but she hadn't wanted to do anything when he was out of routine. Not a good time to set yourself up for a fall.

And talking of doing that, what had she been thinking about last night? Why get into bed with him? *On* the bed, maybe, but *in* it?

Asking for trouble, and she'd got it, with bells on.

He needed you.

And you needed him, every bit as much.

'Josh, come on, let's take these things downstairs and we can go and have breakfast with Grannie and Grandpa!'

'Now?'

She nodded, dredging up a bright smile from somewhere. 'Yes. Look. The farmer's cleared all the snow from the lane. We can get out now, and go to Grannie's house.'

'Bastian come?'

Oh, here we go. 'No, darling. Sebastian lives here.'

'Us live here.'

'No. We can't, Josh. It's not our house, and anyway, we've got a house already.'

He stuck his chin out. 'Want Bastian.'

So did she, but it wasn't going to happen in this lifetime.

She picked up the travel cot, slung the changing bag over her shoulder and pulled up the handle on her case. 'Come on, downstairs, please.'

She trundled the case to the top of the stairs, then picked it up and struggled down the first few steps.

Then a firm hand on her shoulder stopped her, the case was removed from her grasp, the travel cot removed from the other hand and Sebastian carried them down to the kitchen without a word.

'Anything else up there?'

He met her eyes, but warily, and she felt hers skitter away. 'No. That's everything. There's just the train set. I packed it up last night. Oh, and the bag of presents in your room.'

He nodded, went and got everything and returned, putting the train set boxes on the big kitchen table where they seemed to have shared so many important moments in the last few days.

Josh was trailing him, talking to him non-stop, asking if they could live there, if he was coming for breakfast with Grannie, if they were coming back.

He either didn't understand Josh, which was possible, or didn't want to understand, which was much more likely.

'Josh, leave Sebastian alone, we can't stay here and he's not coming with us,' she said softly, and he started to cry.

'Hey. Don't cry, little guy,' Sebastian said, finally relenting and crouching down to Josh's level. 'Mummy's right. You can't stay here, you have to go home to your house, and I can't come with you because I have to stay here in mine.'

'Me stay here,' he said, and he wrapped his arms tightly round Sebastian's neck and hung on.

A pained expression crossed his face for a fleeting second, and he hugged him briefly, but then he gently but firmly disentangled the little boy's arms and prised him away, setting him down on the floor and standing up. 'Come on, Josh, don't cry. You're going to see your Grannie.'

But Josh's arms were wrapped round his legs now, and Georgie unwrapped them and picked him up, sobbing piteously, and Sebastian pushed past her and pulled on his coat and sloshed across to the coach-house to get her car out.

He was gone longer than she expected, but then she heard the car pull up. 'The traction seems fine, the slush is really wet,' he said as he came back in, leaving the car running just by the door. 'The drive's fine and the lane's clear. I just drove down to have a look. You should be OK.'

OK? She doubted it, but she nodded and pulled her coat on, one arm at a time with Josh still in her arms, and then while Sebastian put their luggage in the car, she sat down on a chair to put Josh's coat on.

He wasn't having any of it.

'Come on, Josh,' she pleaded, but he just made it even harder, burrowing into her and hiding his hands, so she carried him out to the car as he was and strapped him in.

'Will he be all right without it?'

'He'll be fine,' she said crisply. 'Look, I think I've got everything but it's really hard with Josh, he carts stuff about all over the place. If you find anything, maybe you could pile it all up and my father could come and collect it.'

He nodded. 'Or I can post it to you.'

'They can do that,' she said, reluctant to give

him her address. She really, really didn't need any more scenes like this one.

And then there was nothing more to say but goodbye, and thank you.

For what?

For opening his home to her, but not his heart?

For making love to her one last time, so she could treasure it in the cold, lonely hours of the nights to come?

For saving her son's life?

'I'll miss you,' he said gruffly. 'Both of you.'

Her eyes flooded with tears, and she nodded. She couldn't speak. Couldn't move. Couldn't do anything except stand there mutely and blink away the stupid, stupid tears—

His thumbs were gentle as he wiped them away.

'Don't cry, George. We're no good for each other.'

But they had been. All this time, the last few days, they'd got on really, really well. Except for the times they hadn't.

She tried to smile, but it was a shaky effort.

'Goodbye, Sebastian. And thank you. For everything.'

Going up on tiptoe, she pressed a gentle, rather wistful kiss to his lips, and then turned and walked out of the door, her head bowed against the rain, her eyes flooding with tears as she left the man she'd never stopped loving standing on the step behind her.

She didn't look back.

He was glad. If she had, he might have weakened, said something.

Like what? Begging her to stay?

He opened the gates remotely from the hall, watched on the security camera as her car turned out of the drive and headed left, the direction the farmer had cleared already.

The car slithered a little, and he frowned. He had his coat on. His keys were in his pocket. He had to make sure she was safe.

He followed her, staying well behind out of sight, and ten minutes later he cruised by the end of her parents' drive.

Her car was there, and her father was carrying her things in, her mother was holding Josh and Georgie was lifting the bag of presents out of the front of the car.

She was safe. Home, and safe.

Duty discharged.

He went home, turned into the drive and saw the soggy remains of the snowman wilting gently on the lawn beside the drive. His nose had fallen out, and one of his eyes, and the scarf had definitely seen better days.

He left it there. It seemed wrong to take it off until the snowman had gone completely, and anyway, it was already ruined.

Everything, he discovered, seemed wrong.

The house, which until Monday had seemed calm and peaceful and a haven, was silent and empty.

The kitchen echoed to his footsteps. The boot room had a little coat, a snuggly jacket and two pairs of wellies missing from it. And under the table was a toy car.

He picked it up, tossing it pensively in his hand. It was a toy Josh might never have played with, if things had been different. If he hadn't been here. If the snow had come a little earlier, or she'd stopped a little later.

If nothing else, Josh and his mother were still alive, they still had each other and they could move on with their lives. And so could he.

Even if the house echoed with every sound he made.

He made some toast and coffee, took it through to the study and paused en route to check the little sitting room.

And saw the Christmas tree, festooned with all the little toys and sticks and fir cones Georgie had made at the kitchen table and Josh had put on the tree.

There were no gingerbread trees or stars left.

Or at least, only one. High up, out of Josh's reach.

He left it there, left it all there and went into the study and phoned his mother.

'Hi. The lane's clear. When do you want to come?'

'Oh. That was quick. Are you all right?'

'Of course I'm all right. Why wouldn't I be?'

'You tell me, darling,' his mother said softly. 'How's Georgie?'

'She's fine. Look, I don't want to talk about this. Are you coming over, or not?'

'Oh, we're coming, whenever you're ready for us. Andrew and Matthew are here, too. Shall we come now?'

'That would be fine. Come as soon as you like.'

'Do you have anything left to eat, or do you want us to get something on the way?'

He gave a slightly strangled laugh. 'There's plenty here. I've got a joint of beef. We can have it for dinner tonight.'

And maybe having a full house would drown out the echoes...

'I knew it.'

'Knew what?'

'That you'd be upset.'

Georgie put the tea towel down on the worktop and rolled her eyes. 'Mum, don't start—'

'Sorry. I'm sorry, but you look so—'

'Mum...'

'OK. Point taken. I'll back off. So—how was your Christmas?'

Wonderful. Heartbreakingly wonderful.

'I don't really want to talk about it,' she said. 'He did us a huge favour, he made a real effort to be nice to Josh who's completely idolised him as you might have guessed, and it's over now and I'd rather just forget it. How was yours?'

'Oh, quiet. We missed you. We were on our own, of course, so I put the turkey in the freezer, but I've got a chicken in the fridge so we could have it for supper or even a late lunch. We've still got most of the trimmings. We could still make it a proper Christmas dinner.'

She forced a smile. She wasn't really hungry, but she owed her mother the courtesy of good manners. 'That would be lovely. Thank you. Want me to peel some potatoes?'

'If you like. It would be nice to have your company, and Josh seems happy enough for now with his Grandpa and the train set.'

Except for the word 'Bastian' that seemed to crop up in every conversation...

He went back to London as soon as his parents and brothers went.

He hadn't intended to, but the empty house was driving him insane, so he loaded up the car with a ton of fresh food out of the pantry and took it to the refuge. He was never going to get through it, so there was no point in wasting it.

He also took back a lot for the office staff, things his PA had over-supplied in her enthusiasm but that would keep until the office reopened and yet more for the refuge. Tash had really overdone it.

And then he went back to work.

He hadn't intended to do that, either, but he was there before the office reopened, sitting at his desk filling his time and his mind with anything rather than Georgie and her apparently rather lovable little boy. Not that there was a lot to do until everyone was back, so in the end he gave up and just walked the streets and went to the theatre and the odd art exhibition, watched the fireworks on New Year's Eve from the window in his apartment and wondered what the New Year would bring.

Nothing he was about to get excited about.

Then he went back into the office at the crack of dawn on the second of January, champing at the bit and ready to get on. Anything rather than this agonising limbo he seemed to be in.

Tash sashayed into his office, humming softly to herself, and stopped dead. 'Hey, boss, what are you doing back? I thought you'd be there till next week. I wasn't expecting you in till Monday.'

He looked up and met his PA's astonished eyes. Her hair was pink this week. Last week it had been orange—or was it the week before? 'It's a bit quiet in the country.'

She frowned, and perched on the edge of his desk, twisting her hair up and anchoring it with a pencil out of the pot.

'Really? I thought you liked that.'

'I do.' He did. He had. Until Georgie came.

'So how was the food? Did you get through it all?'

He laughed. 'Not really. I've brought a lot in for everyone—I thought we could have a sort of random buffet to welcome everyone back.'

He'd got more, too, in the back of the car, but he'd drop that off later at the refuge, to kick the New Year off.

Pity he couldn't seem to kick his year off. Off a cliff, maybe.

'So how was your Christmas?' he asked belatedly.

She gurgled with laughter. Positively gurgled, and flashed a ring under his nose.

He grabbed her hand and held it still, studying the ring in astonishment. 'He did it?'

'He did. In style. Took me to a posh restaurant and went down on one knee and everything.'

He chuckled, and stood up and hugged her. 'I'm really pleased for you, Tash. That's great news.'

Her smile faltered and she pulled a face. 'Yeah. That's the good news.'

'And the bad?' he said, with a sense of impending doom.

'He's got a job offer. He's moving to America for a year—to Chicago—and he wants me to go with him.'

He sat down again, propping his ankle on his knee, his foot jiggling. This was not good news—well, not for him. 'When?'

'As soon as you can replace me.'

He shook his head slowly. 'I'll never be able to replace you, Tash, but you can go as soon as it's right for you. I'll manage.'

'How?'

He grazed his knuckles lightly over her cheek. 'You're not indispensable,' he said gently. 'But I will miss you and there'll always be a place for you here if you want to come back.'

'Oh, Sebastian, I'll miss you, too,' she said, and flung her arms around his neck. 'I wish you could be happy. I hate it that you're so sad.'

'I'm not sad,' he protested, but she gave him a sceptical look.

'Yes, you are. You've been sad ever since I've

known you. You don't even realise it. I don't know who she was, but I'm guessing you've seen her over Christmas, because your eyes look even sadder today.'

He looked away, uncomfortable with her all too accurate analysis.

'Since when were you a psychotherapist?' he asked brusquely, but it didn't put her off. Nothing put Tash off, not when she felt she was on the scent. Maybe it was just as well she was leaving—

'Is she married?'

He gave up. 'No. Not any more.'

'Well, there you are, then. Do you love her? No, don't answer that, it's obvious. Does she love you?'

Did she?

'Yes. But we're not right for each other. Sometimes love's just not enough.'

'Rubbish. It's always enough. Talk to her, Sebastian. I know you. You never talk about anything that matters to you, not really. The only thing you get really worked up about is the refuge, and you never talk about why.'

'It's a good cause.'

She rolled her eyes and pulled the pencil out, shaking her hair down around her shoulders in a shower of shocking pink.

'Go and see her,' she said, stabbing him repeatedly in the chest with the end of the pencil to punctuate every word. 'And talk. *Properly.*'

She dropped the pencil on the desk and swished out of the door. 'Want a coffee before you go?' she asked over her shoulder.

Go? 'Who said anything about going?' he yelled after her, but she ignored him, so he sat down again and stared out of the window at the river.

It was brown with silt from all the run-off after the thaw, and it looked bleak and uninviting.

Like his house.

Was Tash right? Was he sad all the time?

He swallowed hard. Maybe. He hadn't always been. Not while he was with Georgie. She'd taken away the ache, made him feel whole again. And this Christmas, with Josh—he'd been happy.

'Forget the coffee,' he said, snagging his coat off the hook in Tash's office on the way past. 'Don't forget the food. It's in the board room. Share it out. And tell Craig he's a lucky man.'

'Break a leg,' she yelled after him, and he gave a little huff of laughter.

He wasn't really sure what he was doing, and he was far less sure that it would work, but he had to do something, and dithering around for another nine years wasn't going to achieve anything.

It was time to talk to Georgie. Time to tell her the truth in all its ugly glory.

He went home first.

Not to his flat, but to the house.

He'd dropped off the extravagant goodies at the refuge on the way, and wished them all a happy New Year, and then he drove back up to Suffolk and let himself in.

He needed the files, so he could show her. And the test results. Everything.

And then he just had to convince her parents to give him her address in Huntingdon.

It wasn't easy. Her mother was like a Rottweiler, and she wasn't going to give in without a fight.

'Why do you want to see her?'

'I need to talk to her. There are things I need to tell her.'

'You've hurt her.'

He opened his mouth to point out that she'd left him, and shut it. 'I know,' he said after a pause. 'But I want to put it right.'

'How?'

'That's between me and Georgie, Mrs Becket. But I don't want to hurt her, and I especially don't want to hurt Josh.'

'But you will. If you go there, you will.'

'Not if I don't go when he's awake.'

She seemed to consider that for a moment, but then her husband appeared behind her shoulder and frowned at him.

'I don't know whether to shake your hand for saving their lives or punch your lights out,' he growled, and Sebastian sighed.

'Look, this is nothing to do with Christmas. This is about me, and things about me that she doesn't know. Things I should have told her years ago.'

'So why didn't you?' his mother asked.

He shrugged, swallowing hard. 'Because it's not easy.'

She said nothing for a long moment, then gave a shaky sigh.

'It never is easy, making yourself vulnerable. 42 Wincanton Close.'

'Thank you.' He let his breath out slowly, then sucked it in again. 'Don't tell her I'm coming. I don't want her to do anything silly like go out. I'll ring her when I'm there, tell her I want to talk to her, ask if she'll see me. I won't just rock up on the doorstep. Not if she doesn't want me to.'

Her mother nodded. 'Good. Don't hurt her again, Sebastian. Whatever you do, don't hurt her again.'

'Don't worry, Mrs Becket. I won't hurt her. Not intentionally. I love her. I've always loved her.'

'I know that. If I didn't, I wouldn't have given you her address.'

And taking him completely by surprise, she leant forwards and kissed his cheek. 'Good luck.'

He swallowed. 'Thank you. I have a feeling I'll need it.'

'I don't think so. It's been too long coming, but she'll hear you out. She's always been fair.'

He nodded, shook her father's proffered hand and got back in the car. On the seat beside him were a handful of Josh's toys. The car he'd found under the kitchen table. A train carriage, a piece of track, a little wooden tree. And George's shampoo out of the corner of the shower cubicle in her room.

He'd nearly kept it, just in case she kicked him out, because the smell of it reminded him so much of her.

42 Wincanton Close, Huntingdon. He punched it into the satellite navigation system in the car, reversed carefully off their drive and hit the road.

No rush.

He had well over an hour before Josh was in bed, maybe more. Plenty of time to work out what he was going to say.

He laughed at himself.

He'd had years. Nine, for the worst bits. Thirteen for the rest, all the time he'd known her. If he didn't know what to say now, he never would.

'Oh, man up, Corder. She can only kick you out.'

His gut clenched, and he shut his eyes briefly. He didn't need to think about failure. Not now.

He just needed to see her. Everything else would follow.

CHAPTER TEN

HE FOUND THE house easily. It was the one with the 'For Sale' board outside, and the lights were on.

He slowed down to a crawl with a sigh of relief, and looked around.

She was right, it was in a nice neighbourhood. Tree lined roads, pleasant modern detached houses in different styles each with their own garage, arranged at different angles to soften the lines.

Respectable, decent. Safe.

He was glad she was safe. Safe was important.

He drove past, turned round and pulled up not quite opposite the house, where he could see it and she could see him, and spent a moment gathering his thoughts.

Hell, it was hard. His heart was pounding, his mouth felt dry and his gut was so tight it almost hurt.

It was time.

He pulled the phone out of his pocket and dialled her number.

She didn't answer the first time he rang, so he rang again. He knew it was her phone number, because he'd found her phone lying around and she'd got the number stored under 'me'.

He smiled. Predictable George, to keep the same number. All she had to do was pick up.

She didn't, so he sent her a text, and sat and waited.

The text just said, 'Call me' and gave his number, just in case her phone didn't come up with it. Unlikely, but he wasn't giving her any excuses. Not at this point. There was too much riding on it.

And then she rang him, just when he thought she wouldn't.

'Sebastian? What is it? I've had two missed calls from you and a text. What's going on?'

'I need to see you. We need to talk.' He paused, then went on, his voice gruff. 'There are things you should know. Things I should have told you years ago. Well, one thing, really, the only one that really matters.'

There was a second of shocked silence. 'Can you wait an hour? Just until I've fed Josh and got him to bed? We've been out and I'm on the drag.'

He nodded, although she couldn't see him. 'It's kept for thirteen years. It'll keep another hour.'

'I'll call you.'

'Don't bother. I'm outside, in the car. Just flash the porch lights and I'll come over.'

He saw the curtain twitch, and heard her swift intake of breath. 'OK. I'll see you later.'

He was here.

She couldn't believe it. Her heart was thrashing, and yet there was something dawning that could have been hope.

'Josh, do you really want any more of that?' she asked, and he pushed the plate away and shook his head.

'Can I play trains?'

'No. You can have a bath, and I'll read you a

story and you can go to sleep. You've got nursery in the morning and it's late.'

'Want trains,' he said, but he trailed upstairs anyway and sat on the loo on his toddler seat while she ran the bath.

She washed his hair because he'd managed to get ketchup in it, and then she dried him and dressed him in his night nappy and pyjamas, curled up with him on the chair in his room and read him a story, and then snuggled him into his cot.

His eyes were wilting, and before she was out of the door he was asleep.

She gave it five minutes, though, because she didn't want him waking up and interrupting what she instinctively knew was probably the most pivotal conversation of her life.

Cripes.

She went into her bedroom, turned on the bathroom light and studied her face.

She'd been out, and she'd put on a light touch of make-up. Nothing fancy, nothing elaborate, just a touch of eyeshadow and a flick of mascara.

She combed her hair, though, wrestling out the

tangles, and eyed her clothes critically. Jeans, a nice jumper, socks.

Hardly dressed to kill, but if he'd wanted that he would have given her notice. And it really, really didn't matter. Not now. There were far bigger fish to fry.

Her heart in her mouth, she went downstairs and flashed the porch light.

Game on.

He got out of the car, ran a finger round his collar and crossed the road, locking the car as he walked.

The door swung open, and he stopped on the step.

'Are you OK with this?'

She searched his eyes, and nodded. 'Come in. Just don't talk too loudly. He's only just gone down.'

Talk too loudly? Now he was here, he didn't want to talk at all, but that had always been his problem.

She led him into the sitting room, closing the door behind them, and he looked around.

'Nice house.'

'Thank you. Can I get you a drink?'

He was dying of thirst. His mouth felt like the desert. 'Mineral water?'

She nodded and went out, returning a moment later with a bottle and two glasses. She set them down on the coffee table, filled the glasses and then perched on the edge of the sofa, waving her hand at the other end of it.

'Sit down, Sebastian. You're cluttering the place up.'

He sat, clearing his throat, sipping the water.

Wondering where to start…

He's nervous, she realised. It surprised her, and it was somehow comforting. Working on the principle that nature abhorred a vacuum, she didn't speak, supressing the urge to fill the silence in the hope that he would.

He did. He gave a short and utterly humourless laugh, and lifted his head.

'I don't know where to start.'

She shifted closer and took his hand, squeezing it gently, her heart pounding. 'So why don't you start with saying it straight out, whatever it is, like, I'm gay, or I've got cancer, or whatever? And then explain.'

He gave a hollow laugh and his fingers tightened in hers. 'OK. Well, for a start I'm definitely not gay, and as far as I know I don't have cancer. I just—I don't know who I am.'

'What?' She searched his eyes, trying to read them, but they were bleak and empty. Lost. And that scared her. She gripped his hand tighter. 'Sebastian, talk to me.'

He hesitated, then sucked in a breath and said the words that had been dammed up inside him for so long.

'I'm adopted.'

She stared at him. 'You're *what?* When did you find out?'

'When I was seventeen, nearly eighteen. I had no idea until I wanted to get a driving license. We'd never been abroad, I'd never needed a passport, but I wanted to learn to drive, and my parents procrastinated, and then they had to tell me, because I needed my birth certificate and—well, basically it's a fabrication.'

She frowned. 'A fabrication? How?'

He let out a shaky sigh, and his fingers tightened on hers, as if this was the hard bit. 'Because nobody knew anything about me. I was found,' he said carefully. 'In a cubicle, of all places, in the Ladies' room in a department store.'

'Oh, Sebastian! That's so sad. Did they never find your mother? Had she given birth to you in the loos?'

'No, she hadn't just given birth to me. I wasn't a baby. And I was with my mother. She was dead,' he said, his voice hollow. 'Dead, and pregnant, and she'd been beaten up. The cleaner found us in the morning, when the department store opened.'

She pressed a hand to her mouth, the shock rippling through her like an explosion. 'You'd been there *all night*?'

He swallowed, looked away, then looked back at

her, and she could see an echo of the horror lurking in the back of his eyes.

He nodded. 'I must have been. I was two, or
thereabouts.'

'Josh's age,' she whispered, feeling sick.

He nodded again. 'They didn't know exactly,
of course, but they gave me a birth date based on
my calculated developmental age, and the place of
birth is the town where I was found. They never
managed to identify my mother. No woman answering her description was ever reported missing, and nobody's looked for her since. She had
no ID of any sort on her, no handbag, no wallet.
Nothing.'

She didn't know what to say. Shock held her
rigid, and it was long seconds before she started
to breathe again, short, shaky breaths of horror.
She rested her head on his shoulder, and his other
hand came up and cradled it tight. She could feel
the tremors running through him, the shaking of
his hand, the jerky breaths.

What on earth had he gone through in those
long, dark hours? She thought of her baby, her pre-

cious, darling baby, trapped alone with her dead body in a public toilet cubicle, and silent tears cascaded down her cheeks. She lifted her free hand and found his jaw, cradled it in her palm, turned her head and kissed him.

His tears mingled with hers, and for a long time they sat there holding each other, cheek to cheek, just letting the shockwaves die away. Then he eased away from her and scrubbed his face with his hands, swiping away the tears and sucking in much-needed air.

'My parents didn't tell me that all at once. They just told me I was adopted, that I'd been found and nobody knew who my mother was. I assumed she'd abandoned me, so I spent three years hating her, and three years hating my parents for not telling me, for letting me think I was theirs. And then I found out the truth. The whole, ugly, sordid truth, and other things started to make sense. The dreams I'd had all my life. The claustrophobia, the fear of being in a tight space in the dark.'

'Which is why you freaked out when you were in the attic with Josh.'

He nodded. 'I heard your footsteps coming, and I said to Josh, "Shh, don't make a sound," and we held our breath, and suddenly I had this rush of—I don't know. Memory? Or just an overworked imagination? But it suddenly seemed so real, as if I recognised the words. And I hear it in my dreams, someone telling me to hush, and the footsteps, and hidden in there with his tiny body next to mine— I just had to get the hell out. Was he all right?'

'Yes, he was fine, but I wondered what on earth had happened. I knew about your claustrophobia, but it looked—I don't know. Worse. You looked awful, but you wouldn't talk to me.'

'I couldn't. I'm sorry. I find it really hard to talk about. And I couldn't talk then, apparently. I didn't talk until I was nearly three—or what they'd decided was nearly three, although apparently I might have been younger. They kept a growth chart and you're supposed to be half your adult height at two, and I wasn't half my current height until I was supposedly two and five months, so I was probably younger than they thought when I was found.'

'So maybe not even talking at that point.'

'No. But I was silent, George. It wasn't just that I didn't talk, I didn't cry, or laugh, or babble. I didn't make a sound—and telling Josh to shush—did she tell me not to make a sound? My mother? Probably, because shut in there with Josh it all felt terrifyingly familiar, so maybe I was just too afraid to speak in case something else bad happened.'

Poor, poor little boy. She shook her head slowly, rubbing the back of his hand with her thumb, slowly, rhythmically, her heart aching for him. Oh, Sebastian…

'So what happened to you, after you were found? Where did you go?'

'My parents fostered me. I was put with them straight away, and they moved heaven and earth to adopt me, and gradually I grew more confident and turned into a normal, healthy child, but they never told me. All those years I thought I was theirs, all those birthday parties that weren't my birthday at all, and then this huge hole opened up underneath me, this void where I'd had security and certainty and a sense of history, of belonging. And it was all a lie. It was only later I learned there had been even more lies, covering up the bits of the truth that even then they didn't feel they could tell me.'

Her fingers tightened on his. 'They weren't lying to you, Sebastian. They were protecting you. Doing what they felt was best.'

'I know. I know that, and I know they love me, and don't get me wrong, I love them, too, and I'm deeply grateful for everything they've done for me, but—I'm not theirs, and I thought I was, and that really hurts. If they'd told me the truth, right from the beginning, that my mother was dead and that they didn't know who she was, then it wouldn't have been such a shock when I heard it.'

'So when did you find out about your mother? Was that when you changed, when you went so funny on me? You said three years after you first realised you were adopted, so you would have been—what? Twenty? Nearly twenty-one?'

He nodded. 'Yes. And I just retreated into myself.'

'Why didn't you tell me?' she asked, desolate

now that he'd carried this all alone for so long. 'Oh, Sebastian, why didn't you tell me? You should have trusted me. I would have understood.'

'Because I didn't want anything to change. I felt that you were the only person who loved me for myself. You weren't hiding a guilty secret from me, you had no obligation to me, and I was afraid to tell you in case it changed things. That's why I bought the house, because the time I spent there with you was the happiest time of my life.'

He looked down at her, his eyes tender. 'I fell in love with you there, on our first date, when you took me there and showed it to me.'

'That wasn't a date!'

'Yes, it was. I knew Jack wasn't going to be around, and you'd always been friendly towards me. I'd just found out I was adopted, and I needed to get out, give myself time for it all to sink in. And there you were, in a skimpy little top and shorts, your skin kissed by the sun, and when you suggested we went out for the bike ride I thought all my Christmases had come at once.'

'It *was* just a bike ride.'

'No. It was you showing me your secret hide-away, letting me into your dreams, sharing your fantasies, and we made fantasies of our own. I was still reeling from the news that I was adopted, and it was an escape from it, a different reality. In the next few weeks it became our own world, somewhere safe that I could go. And suddenly it all seemed plausible. If I could get rich enough, so I could afford it, we could buy the house and live there and found our dynasty, yours and mine, and I would have a real family, my own flesh and blood.'

She touched his cheek, wiping away the last trace of their tears. 'You should have told me, Sebastian.'

He looked away, his face bleak, and she let her hand fall.

'I know, but I didn't want to change things. You knew who you were. You look like your parents. You're part of them, they're part of you. And I don't have that. My brothers do—they aren't adopted. Nature seemed to have sorted itself out for my parents by that point, and there's no question that Matt and Andy are theirs, but not me. For me, my identity, my origins, even my nationality will always be a mystery. I'm a cuckoo in the nest, Georgie, and I never forget how much I owe them, but they should have told me.'

'They had their reasons. Maybe they thought it would hurt you more? It must have been really traumatic—you were hardly more than a baby, but much more aware than a baby would have been. The impact must have been horrific, and they would have wanted to protect you.'

'I know. Logically, I know, but I didn't feel logical. Suddenly I didn't belong, and that was so shocking to me. It rocked me to my foundations. And when I found out the rest, when I saw my adoption file and the police file, and it was so sordid and harsh, it was even worse. How could I tell you that? I didn't want to distress or disgust you—'

'Disgust me? It wouldn't have disgusted me!'

'I didn't know that. I still don't know that. She could have been anyone, George. She could have been a prostitute or a drug addict, a murderer, even—'

'She was somebody's *daughter*,' she said, appalled that he could think that she was so shallow that his mother's plight would put her off him. 'However she ended up there, she was just a girl—how old was she?'

He shrugged. 'Early twenties, they thought, maybe younger?'

Her eyes flooded again. 'Poor, poor girl. She must have been so terrified. And she must have loved you—she tried to protect you, shut you away in a public place where a man couldn't get to you without drawing attention to himself, and it cost her her life.'

He nodded slowly. 'Yes, it did. And I'd spent three years hating her for something she hadn't done. I didn't realise how much it had changed me, thinking I'd been abandoned, that she hadn't loved me enough to keep me. Why not? What kind of vile child had I been that I wasn't I lovable? But then I heard the truth, and I just needed to find out all I could about her, but there's nothing. I still don't know who she was, and nobody's launched any kind of official search for anyone answering her description in all this time.'

'What about DNA?' she asked, finally on solid ground. 'I know it can't tell you much, but it can tell you something about where you're from.'

'Northern Europe, probably England. No more than that. And if nobody's looked, then the trail's lost and I'll never know who she was, or who I am. And that's the worst thing. I have no idea who I really am. My name, my place and date of birth—not even what nationality I am. Just speculation, all of it.'

'No! You *know* who you are,' she said fiercely. 'And *I* know who you are. I've always known. It wouldn't have made any difference to me where you'd come from, what you were called, what date you were born. You were you, and you've always been you, and it's you I loved. You should have *told* me, Sebastian. You should have trusted me.'

He turned his head slowly and looked at her, his eyes bleak. 'But I did trust you. And you left me.'

She opened her mouth to argue, but then shut it

again, because it was true. She had left him. She'd walked away and left him, when she'd promised to love him forever.

Well, that hadn't been a lie. She loved him still, but she'd left him when he'd needed her the most, and it tore her apart.

'I'm so sorry,' she said brokenly. 'I had no idea what you were going through. I wish you'd told me, shared it with me. I would never have left you if I'd known. I loved you so much, I've always loved you. You're a good man, and you always have been, and you must never doubt that—look what you did for Josh and me over Christmas—but still you didn't let us into your heart. You gave us so much, and you didn't need to do that, but you held yourself back like you always do, because everyone you've ever loved has let you down, haven't they, one way or another? No wonder you don't trust your feelings or give your heart to anyone, least of all me.'

'I gave my heart to you,' he said quietly. 'I gave it to you thirteen years ago, and you still have it. That offer stands.'

She shook her head. 'But I left you. I don't deserve it.'

'Yes, you do. I was a nightmare. I know that. But I needed you, and I loved you, and I still do, Georgia. And I know you love me. What I don't know is if you can forgive me, or if you can live with a man from nowhere.'

'Oh, Sebastian. Of course I can forgive you. And whether or not I can live with you is nothing to do with where you've come from so much as where you're going and how. That was what changed. That was the problem, the thing I couldn't live with.'

'I know. I'm sorry. But there was a reason I was so driven.'

'A reason you didn't share with me!'

'I know. I should have.'

'You should. I could have helped you with the DNA research. It's my field, Sebastian. I might have been able to find out more.'

'I doubt it. I've paid a fortune for the best advice—'

'The best isn't necessarily commercially available. And I'm on the inside. Don't overlook that.'

He nodded. 'I won't. But it can't alter the way I was then, how driven I was—still am. After I found out what had actually happened to my mother, the emphasis changed. I needed to make more money—much more, not for me, but to make sure it couldn't happen again, that there'd be somewhere safe for women to go. I support various charities, for women and children who are victims of domestic violence, and I set up a refuge which I fund and maintain. I had to, to stay sane. I couldn't just let it go, and it was eating me up, but now I'm doing something, and making a difference, and I feel I've got my priorities right.'

'You have. You've settled down.'

'Grown up?' he said drily, and she laughed.

'Probably. I prefer to think you've developed a more mature and balanced perspective. And I have, too, so before you start worrying, I'm sure I can live with you now even if I couldn't then.'

'You can?'

'Of course I can—and I could have done then if

you'd shared this with me. I think it's a fabulous cause, and I would have supported you and worked with you on it, but you never gave me a chance.'

His eyes were filled with shadows. 'I know. I'm sorry. I just didn't know how to say it, and the longer it went on, the harder it got. And after you went I was so hurt and angry that you'd left me, there was no way I was going to tell you. Then I heard you were married, and I thought you'd moved on.'

'No. I'll never move on from loving you. I've loved you for thirteen years—I fell in love with you on that first date, too, and I promised to love you forever. That hasn't changed, even though I couldn't stay with you then. I still love you. I've never stopped loving you.'

'Even though you were married to David?'

She shrugged. 'He was a nice man, and we were both lonely. You wouldn't let me in, you'd done nothing but shut me out for months. Years later, you still hadn't contacted me again and I had no reason to suppose you ever would. And if we hadn't been snowed in together this Christmas, I don't know that that would have ever changed.'

'No. Maybe not. As I said, I just assumed you'd moved on.'

'Only in a way. Not in my heart. It was a compromise, a rationalisation, and I can't regret it because it's given me Josh, but it was only ever a way of finding a measure of happiness. You were my first love, my only true love, but I was never going to have you, and I didn't want to be alone, and if David hadn't died, we would have been together forever. But he did die, and we're talking, at last, and maybe finally sorting out what we should have sorted out years ago.'

She reached up and cradled his cheek in her hand. 'I love you, Sebastian. And if you're asking me to marry you, the answer's yes.'

'I asked you years ago.'

'No, you didn't. You promised me we'd be together forever, and we talked about being married, but I don't believe you ever asked me.'

He gave a soft laugh, and eased off the sofa,

landing on one knee at her feet. He took her hand in his and stared up into her eyes with a wry smile.

'Georgia Becket Pullman, I love you now as much as I've ever loved you, more than life itself. Without you I'm nothing. With you, I can conquer the world. Marry me. Have my children, to keep your little Josh company and give him a whole host of brothers and sisters. Our dynasty. My very own, real family.'

His smile faded, and his eyes grew bright.

'Marry me, George? Please?'

Her eyes filled. 'Oh, Sebastian—of course I'll marry you! I've already said yes.'

'You made me ask you,' he accused.

'Only because I wanted to hear you say it,' she laughed, but the laugh hiccupped into a sob, and she slid off the sofa onto her knees and went into his arms, hugging him tight to her heart, aching for the little boy he'd been and the strong, courageous man he'd become.

He shifted onto the sofa, lifting her easily onto his lap and cradling her close. 'It's a pity you've got a job,' he said.

She tilted her head and peered at him. 'Why? It might be useful to you in the future, trying to track your family. I've got all the right contacts.'

A week ago, that would have made his heart race faster. Now, he found he didn't care, because he had the only thing that could ever matter this much to him.

"I could still use your skill and expertise now,' he said.

'Why?'

He smiled. 'Because my PA's leaving. She's getting married and moving to Chicago, and I'll need someone to fill in until I can replace her. But that's only short term. Long term, of course, we've got a dynasty to work on. Maybe you'd better warn your boss.'

She laughed and rested her head on his shoulder. 'Yes, I better had. The first little Corder is due on the nineteenth of September.'

He went utterly still, and then he gave a shaky, incredulous laugh and hugged her tight. 'Really? You're having my baby?'

'It would seem so. I did the test this morning. It was very faint, but it was positive.'

'Wow.' He laughed again. 'I didn't even think—that night, when I had the dream?'

'When else? There was only the once.'

'And you're sure? The test can't be wrong?'

'No. You can have a false negative, but never a false positive. I deliberately got a very sensitive test kit.'

'Have you told your mother?'

She shook her head. 'No. Not before you. I was trying to work out how to tell you, but I knew you'd go all Neanderthal and insist on marrying me, so I really wanted to talk to you first and get you to open up to me so I'd know you wanted it for the right reasons.'

'And I came to you. You'd better thank Tash for that. She said she wished I wasn't always sad. I said I wasn't. She pointed out that I was. I am. I have been for years, and the only time I'm not sad is when I'm with you.

'It's like you said to me once, when you were talking about David. He was a nice man, and you loved him, but you didn't feel as if you couldn't breathe if he wasn't there. As if there was no co-lour, no music, no poetry. No sense to your life. That's how I feel when I'm with you. As if my life has colour and music and poetry, and it all makes sense, and after you'd gone everything was grey and empty and silent. It took Tash to point it out to me.'

'You *really* owe her a bonus now.'

He laughed and hugged her closer. 'I tell you what, they're going to have a cracker of a wed-ding present.'

'Good. I hope we get invited to the wedding. I want to thank her.'

'That's easy.' He pulled his phone out of his pocket, hit a speed dial number and smiled. 'Tash? My fiancée would like a word with you.'

EPILOGUE

'HAPPY CHRISTMAS, Mrs Corder?'

His arms slid round her from behind, his chin resting on her shoulder. She felt his lips nuzzle her ear, and she laughed and leaned back into him.

'*Very* Happy Christmas, Mr Corder.' She turned in his arms with a smile, and found it reflected in his eyes. 'Where's Evie?'

'Sleeping. On my mother.'

'Not mine, then.'

'For a change, not,' he said with a lazy smile. 'Come and sit down. You've done enough in the kitchen today.'

'I've hardly done anything,' she protested as he towed her down the hall. 'You wouldn't let me.'

'You're a nursing mother.'

'Yes. Not an invalid.'

He smiled indulgently. 'Humour me. I like looking after you. I've got a lot of years to catch up on. So, how do you think it's going?'

'Christmas? Brilliantly. Nobody's had a fight yet, everyone's enjoyed the food—'

'I should hope so. I let Tash loose on the ordering again, remember.'

She chuckled. 'Yes. She's good at it. Impeccable taste.'

'She just knows what I like.'

'So modest.'

He gave a soft huff of laughter and hugged her closer to his side. From down the hall they could hear the hubbub of conversation, interspersed with laughter and the occasional raised voice as someone tried to put their point.

The family were all gathered in the drawing room in front of a roaring fire, playing silly games and getting over the monumental feast that had been Christmas lunch. There wasn't room in the smaller sitting room for all of them, and even the enormous dining table had been filled to capacity.

The house was straining at the seams, all ten bedrooms occupied. Both sets of parents had come to share the celebrations, together with her brother Jack and his wife and two children, Sebastian's brothers Andy and Matt and their girlfriends, and Tash and Craig, who were honorary family members. Including them and Josh and Evie, that made eighteen—nineteen if you counted Tash's burgeoning bump. Twenty-one if you counted the dog and cat.

Not bad for a start at family life, she thought contentedly.

He pulled her to a halt in the hall, next to the Christmas tree. It was decorated with last year's stock cube parcels and bundles of twigs, fresh gingerbread trees and stars and little home-made angels that dangled around the lower branches.

The sophisticated glass baubles were safely near the top of the tree, glinting in the light from the enormous crystal chandelier that hung above it, and it looked wonderful.

She sighed happily. 'What a lovely tree.'

'Isn't it?'

He glanced up, and there overhead, dangling

from the landing bannisters above, was a sprig of mistletoe.

'Well, now, would you look at that?' he murmured, his eyes twinkling with mischief, and threading his hands into her hair, he lowered his head and kissed her...

* * * * *